Lady of the Wye

Frances Powell

This is a work of fiction. Names, characters, places and incidents either are products of the author's imagination or are used fictitiously. Any resemblance to actual events, locales or persons, living or dead, is entirely coincidental.

Other novels by Frances Powell

> The Bodyguard

> Mystery of White Horse Lake

A Ballysea Mystery Series:

> The O'Brien

> A Bad Wind Blowing

> The O'Brien: The Untold Story

Cover Design by: Jo Stallings

This book is dedicated to Mrs. Sue Parslow for graciously showing me around her beautiful home, Wilton Castle, and the town and people of Ross-on-Wye that have brought me so much pleasure over the years.

Chapter 1

It was idyllic…the perfect place for a picnic.

Nothing could be more relaxing than sitting on the riverbank listening to birdsong and the gentle lapping of the water against the willow-lined shore. That was until she floated by, with the sleeves of her gown spread wide like the gossamer wings of a butterfly, interrupting their cucumber sandwiches and pitcher of Pimms.

Nothing usually happened in the quiet market town that had grown up centuries ago along the shores of the River Wye. Other than a few Friday night disturbances at the local pubs, the town was quiet and had remained virtually unchanged for generations. The town seemed to have been caught in some type of time warp. If you stripped away the modern cars and compared a photo of the same street a hundred years ago, you would find little, if anything, changed. And that's how he liked it.

Change and Chief Inspector Fergus were not, shall we say, on the very best of terms.

It was, indeed, the perfect place for the recently transferred London detective to slow down his duties as he eased into retirement. It was why he had chosen the Herefordshire town when the vacancy notice was posted.

Everything was, in fact, nearly perfect until that lazy summer afternoon when the Lady of the Wye surfaced.

Chapter 2

Chief Inspector Cameron Fergus had come up through the ranks since moving from his small hometown north of Edinburgh to the bustling metropolis on the Thames. His childhood home in Scotland lay north of Falkirk on the banks of the River Firth. Airth was the perfect place for the quiet, young, ginger-haired boy to grow into manhood. In truth, the most exciting thing that ever happened there was the Highland Games in July every year when the population of less than two thousand more than tripled in size. It was during these games, Cameron or Cam, as his mother called him, was able to earn a bit of money by working the various stalls when young, and then when older by giving ghost tours of the haunted castle. Cam would describe in hushed tones the sightings of the beautiful young nanny and her two small charges who died in a fire at the castle. In all reality, she was neither young nor beautiful but it made for a more enticing story and Cam soon realized the better the story, the bigger the tip at the end of the tour. Cam would jump dramatically, as if bitten by some invisible creature, as he warned those on the tour of the ghost dog that roamed the hallways enjoying a nibble at unsuspecting guests' ankles. The rest of the year was spent attending school and picking up whatever odd jobs he could find to help his widowed mother make ends meet. They had just enough land to grow a few vegetables and raise chickens for their table and for sale at the town market. Even though times were tough for mother and son, they were happy times for Cam in their small cottage by the river.

All this was to change in the winter of his seventeenth year when his mother contracted pneumonia and died. With no family left, Cam sold their small holding farm, packed his bags, took one last look at the river he had grown to love and moved south to London.

The gentle sound of water lapping against the shoreline always had a calming effect on Cam. As a child it was the last thing he could recall hearing every night right before falling asleep, so it came as no surprise he would seek out a place close to the mighty Thames for his first home in London. Since arriving in London he had been renting a room from a former school teacher's aunt close to the station where he was assigned after completing his police training. It was on his walk to work along the shores of the Thames he first spotted her. She was older than what he was normally attracted to and a bit dirty and worn around the edges but he figured she would do nicely for his needs. He had simple needs, after all, and with a little elbow grease the old boat would clean up nicely.

She was just an old narrow boat but moored in a quiet residential area within walking distance to work, close enough to restaurants and corner shops to take care of his daily needs and more importantly, the price was right. He had saved enough from the sale of their Scottish home to pay cash for the boat and still have enough left over to do the complete restoration, as long as he was careful and did most of the work himself. Cam didn't mind spending all his off-hours working on his boat. After all, he knew very few people in London, and as for his work colleagues; they were far from welcoming to the new recruit. Cam didn't really care. He had grown used to being called "ginger" since first moving to London but had hoped things would've been different with his fellow officers, but they were not. Evening comradery at the local pub after shifts never included Cam but that was alright with Cam since it gave him plenty of time to outfit his new floating home and study for every upcoming promotion exam.

Once the outside of the boat was painted during the dry autumn, Cam turned his attention to refurbishing and decorating the interior. The entire interior was made of the most beautiful honey-colored wood, the floors, walls and ceiling… all wood. It had taken Cam the better part of three weeks working in all his off-hours to clean and polish the wood to a high gloss. Once he was finished, he set out for Camden Market and purchased some second-hand rugs to protect the floor's finish. Throughout the long winter, Cam searched second-hand furniture shops and street markets hunting for bargains to furnish his home.

He was an old-fashioned soul and finally settled on a small, traditional loveseat and a Queen Anne chair which completely filled his long and narrow lounge. The loveseat was worn and tatty much like Cam and his mother had in their home in Airth, but like his mother, Cam knew how to tart it up. The very next day off, he went back to the market and searched through the stalls until he found the perfect white bedspread to cover the loveseat. He had already made up his mind the chair was to be covered in the tartan pattern of his beloved Scotland and he bought enough fabric to cover not only the chair but also to make two pillows for the loveseat. On the same trip, he ventured upon a rather tarnished brass floor lamp that was a little worse for wear but still serviceable. Once all his purchases were complete, Cam stopped at his local curry house for a Chicken Korma take-away and hurried home arriving just as snow flurries began to drift slowly from the gray winter sky. Pulling the lids off the cartons, the spicy aromas of ginger, garlic and cardamom mixed with coconut sauce filled the whole boat with the most tantalizing aromas. Dishing the chicken and sauce over the basmati rice on one of the only two plates he owned, Cam broke off a piece of the fragrant Naan bread and scooping up the curry tucked into his dinner. For a young man as thin as he was he had a veracious appetite and thanks to being a regular customer at the local curry house, Mr. Singh, the owner, made sure Cam was given the largest of portions. Mr. Singh rationalized that having a police officer living mere steps away from his front door as a regular customer provided his restaurant with an aura of security.

Once dinner was over and his lone dish washed, Cam settled into his habit of spending a couple hours reading before bed. The second-hand bookstalls at the local markets allowed Cam to collect enough interesting books to hold him through the worst of the cold weather. He rested now because once spring arrived the country farmer in him hoped to grow some vegetables in containers on the deck.

It was at these very bookstalls he met Helen, the woman who was to become his wife a year later. Like Cam, she had only recently moved to London and had a love of books. Growing up in the Welsh borders with her family, Helen had found it necessary to move to the capitol to pursue her writing career. It was Helen who finally, nearly twenty years later, gently nudged Cam into the eventual move to Ross-on-Wye, after their children were grown and they had no need for the large family home they had moved to in Richmond when the children were young. With their son living in New Zealand and their daughter living in Canada with her husband and children, there was no longer any reason to stay in the capitol. The move would also make it much easier to visit her brothers and sisters in nearby Wales.

After living in rented accommodations in a rural location outside Ross for six months the couple was delighted when a former guest house on Wye Street came on the market. The characterful seven bedroom house was larger than the two empty-nesters either needed or wanted, but the price was right and the location ideal. Cam's love of water and the views of the meandering River Wye, which could be viewed from the sitting room, dining room and no less than three bedrooms, was enough to get the seller the full asking price. There was enough of a small garden to allow Helen to putter about in and it even offered a patio with more stunning river views. Although Helen would have preferred a more rural location, she had to agree with Cam being in walking distance to everything she needed was ideal.

For Cam, it was a quick ten minute walk up the High Street and across Church Street to his office with the West Mercia Police on Old Maid's Walk.

After dinner a week after moving into their new town home in Ross, Helen laughed as she asked, "So, the station is on Old Maid's Walk, huh? I guess there must have been a few old maids in town."

Taking a sip of his after-dinner coffee and settling himself on the sofa, the normally very serious Cam began to chuckle as he replied, "I asked that very same thing the first day at the station and Sergeant Roberts explained the history of the street name to me, but I'm not sure you'll want to hear it this soon after you've finished your meal."

Topping-up her wine glass with the remainder of the white wine, Helen said, "Go on then. You've got my curiosity up now."

"Alright, if you're sure if won't upset you."

Dropping down on the sofa next to her husband and cuddling up under his outstretched arm, Helen replied, "I'll be fine, after all I am under police protection."

"Well, if you are certain," replied Cam placing a kiss on his wife's forehead.

"During the 17th century, Mr. Markey, the wealthy owner of Alton Court hired a young and handsome gardener named Ralph Mortimer. It seems Ralph secretly fell in love with his employer's beautiful second daughter, Clara, and she with him. Because of class distinction, old man Markey wasn't going to approve the marriage and arranged for his daughter to marry another high class landowner. Needless to say, Clara was upset but poor Ralph was so distraught he committed suicide."

Resting her head on Cam's shoulder, Helen sighed, "How horrible."

Standing and pointing out the window at the Wye, he continued, "That's not the worse bit. They found him floating out there and being the superstitious lot they were in those days, they took his body to the intersection of Alton and Copse Cross Street after sunset and drove a stake through his heart before burying him in a secret, unmarked grave to ensure he wouldn't rise from his grave and bite people as they slept."

Shaking her head, Helen said, "How gruesome, but it still doesn't explain why they call it Old Maids Walk."

"Oh, there is more. A few days later as Clara was walking down the aisle to wed the man her father had chosen for her, she collapsed and fell into a trance before the wedding ceremony could be completed. She was taken home only to vanish a short time later. She was found wandering aimlessly on Alton Road searching for Ralph's grave. At every opportunity she would escape the house to make the trip up and down the lane to Copse Cross Street. She continued this for decades until her death put an end to her wandering. And that's why the street was named Old Maids Walk."

"That's so sad. Do you really suppose it's true?" asked Helen.

"According to written history from the period, it is. I dare say, we are much more civilized these days."

"Well thank goodness for that. I'm sure you miss all the excitement of working in London but as for me, I'm glad we moved here and the worst thing you have to deal with is petty crimes, no grisly murders to keep you working day and night."

Hugging his wife, Cam smiled down at her and said, "Tomorrow is my day off. How about a picnic on the riverbank?" asked Cam.

As the two made their way upstairs to bed, across the river a body was being silently dragged down a grassy slope and rolled into the river.

Chapter 3

Helen was the first to see her. She had just poured herself her second glass of Pimms and was watching a mother duck bringing her ducklings downstream when her eyes were drawn to something white half submerged in the water.

Squinting her eyes to get a clearer look at the object, she suddenly jumped up from the blanket knocking over the rest of the pitcher of Pimms on a napping Cam.

"Helen, for God's sake what's wrong? Are you quite alright?" asked Cam as he noticed the look of horror on his wife's ashen face.

Helen just stood and pointed, unable to speak. She couldn't manage a word until finally she blurted out, "Body!"

Cam was looking in the direction of Helen's pointed finger when the undergrowth holding the partially submerged body gave way with the rushing current and the body of the woman began floating downstream. Jumping to his feet, Cam began to wade out into the river and was just able to grab hold of a piece of clothing before the current took the body out of reach. Dragging the body toward the shore, Cam shouted to his wife, "Helen, call 999!"

Helen had already called the emergency services number as soon as she saw her husband wade out into the Wye and help was on the way. By the time Cam dragged the body to the bank of the river the sounds of screaming sirens could be heard coming from all directions.

Cam had seen enough victims of drowning in the Thames, both accidental and suicide, during his years in London and knew from one glimpse it wouldn't be necessary to check for a pulse. As he waited for SOCO to arrive he knelt over the body and began to mentally make notes of his observations. The victim was female and young, probably no older than her mid-twenties. She was slight of build with shoulder length hair and delicate features. She was dressed in a long white flowing dress of what appeared to be made of cotton fabric. She wore no jewelry. No sign of a wedding band. From the condition of her body, she hadn't been in the water long. No obvious sign of trauma.

As Cam rose to his feet, Helen wrapped the blanket they had moments before been enjoying their picnic on around Cam's shoulders and said, "Such a pretty young girl. Do you think she killed herself?"

"We'll have to wait for the medical examiner's report but I don't see any obvious signs of trauma. It could be accidental or suicide. But until we know for sure, it's still a suspicious death. We need to identify the victim first and notify her family so we can get a formal identification."

Slipping her arms around her husband's wet waist, Helen replied, "How horrible for the family."

Glancing across the river upstream from where the victim had surfaced, Cam asked the first arriving patrolman, Sergeant Roberts, "What's over there?"

"Wilton Castle, sir," replied the young Sergeant as he looked away from the young victim and turned his attention to his Chief Inspector.

"Do you recognize the victim, Sergeant?" asked Cam as he continued to stare at the battlement ruins.

"No sir. I've never seen her before."

Nodding and rubbing his chin, Cam thought, 'If she was local then surely Roberts would recognize her, having grown up in the area and lived here all his life.'

"Well then Sergeant, I'll wait here for SOCO to arrive if you'll drive my wife home and then check all the local guest houses and hotels in the area. See if anyone matching the victim's description is registered there."

It wasn't long before the locally assigned forensic pathologist arrived. Mary Hamilton was a large-boned country woman who had previously been a practicing small animal veterinarian. Unfortunately, just two years into her practice she developed a severe allergy to her patients. It was then she switched to pathology. Mary had been the first member of the team to stop by, bringing a welcome basket when Helen and Cam moved into their new home, and she and Helen had become great friends, often meeting for coffee in town.

Walking over and stooping down beside the already squatting Mary, Cam asked, "What do you think, Mary?"

Mary had grown very fond of the newly arrived Chief Inspector, as he treated her with the same professionalism he did all the other officers. He was a no-nonsense investigator, just like her.

"Hard to tell Cam, until I get her on the slab but from initial examination, I see no obvious signs of trauma. Pretty little thing, isn't she? Wonder what made her do it?"

Cam straightened up and turned his attention back to the castle remains across the river before replying, "So you're assuming it's a suicide?"

"Very possibly Cam, but like I said, I'll be able to tell more after the post-mortem. I should have the results for you by later tomorrow," replied Mary.

Standing up, Mary's eyes followed the direction of Cam's stare and said, "That's Wilton Castle. Have you ever been there?   You should take Helen over when the roses are in bloom. They're simply beautiful. Nothing compares to the floral scents of those roses. The owners have spent the last fifteen years restoring the manor house and the ruins with the help of the National Trust. It's truly a magical place," said Mary with a faraway look in her eyes.

Noticing a woman walking her black Labrador on the opposite shore, Cam asked, "So they have been there fifteen years, huh?"

As Mary finished zipping the victim in the body bag, she placed her hand on the small of her back and slowly straightened up, stretching her aging back, then looked across the river to the castle and replied, "Because of the dangerous condition of the Elizabethan manor house, they've only been able to live there for the last ten years.   That's the owner now, Mrs.

23

Parsons, and her dog Bella. Bella used to be a favorite patient of mine. And Mrs. Parsons, she's a real lady and quite a dog lover, too. She could have drowned out there in the currents when she went in to save Bella when she was a wee pup. Now that's a really special lady, in my book."

Cam nodded as he watched the obviously aging Labrador as she stayed right by her mistress' side, then said, "I'll probably be calling on them later today. I'll pass along your regards."

"Thanks Cam. I've been meaning to stop by for a visit but things have been hectic at the farm lately."

Mary owned a small farm near Lydbrook, just a short distance from Ross, where she kept sheep and chickens. She was always dropping off fresh eggs to Helen in exchange for some of Helen's delicious baked goods.

Cam could never quite understand how a woman as soft-hearted and gentle as Mary could handle the depressing and obviously gruesome work of autopsying a victim. Unable to control his curiosity any longer, he asked, "Mary, how do you deal with working with dead bodies all the time?"

"Much the same as you I guess, Cam."

"Well, at least I don't see corpses every day. Most days it's only petty crime," replied Cam.

Looking back at Cam with a smile, Mary replied, "Honestly, I really enjoy the work. It's like solving a mystery and I've always loved a good mystery."

Chapter 4

Cam stood gazing across the river for a few minutes longer after Mary left with the body of the unidentified victim. Usually, the sound of the water lapping against the shore calmed Cam, but not today. Today, he felt only anger. The poor girl wasn't much younger than his daughter, who he missed terribly since she emigrated with her husband to Canada. Cam pushed the tall weeds down with his still-soaking trainers and thought to himself how he had been really fond of his son-in-law until he had accepted the promotion that prompted the move to Canada and he had taken with him Cam's daughter and grandchildren. He had just muttered, "Selfish bastard,' under his breath when SOCO arrived.

"Who sir?" asked the young coverall-clad officer who had come up from behind without Cam hearing his approach.

"Oh sorry, my mind was a thousand miles away. Officer Parker isn't it?" asked Cam.

"Yes sir, kind of you to remember," replied a smiling Sam Parker. Sam was amazed the Chief Inspector would remember his name after only one brief meeting, but he had heard a number of fellow officers commenting on the man's brilliant memory. Cam had come to West Mercia Police with an outstanding record at the Met. Being a stranger to the area, there was a lot of skepticism about the new Chief Inspector but within weeks, all doubts had been laid to rest. Cam Fergus was a brilliant detective, a fair boss, and what the lads called "a man's man."

Cam looked around the riverbank before turning back to Sam Parker and pointing to his left remarked, "I pulled the body of the deceased from the river to the bank here. My wife and I were enjoying a picnic on my day off when my wife spotted something entangled in the undergrowth close to the other shore so I think we can best use your resources over on the other side of the river."

Sam nodded in agreement and said, "Over at the Castle, sir? I haven't been there since I was a young lad. An elderly lady owned it at the time. Kept to herself, she did. I must say, it looks much improved since then."

Cam looked over at the young baby-faced officer who didn't appear to be far into his twenties himself and smiled as he wondered actually how old the serious young man was.

"I'll go ahead Officer Parker. You can follow with your team in about an hour," said Cam as he looked down at his wrist watch and made note of the time.

"I'll need to speak to the owners so they understand why we want access to their property. Why don't you and the lads get some tea or coffee and meet me there. You may need it. It looks like it may be a long evening."

"Yes sir. Thank you. Can we bring a cuppa for you?"

"No thanks, Officer Parker. I live just up the way and I'm going to slip home and get out of these wet clothes, shower and dress. I'll have a cup while I'm making myself look presentable," replied Cam as he looked down at his mud and grass-stained clothes.

"We'll cordon off the area with crime scene tape to keep any curious locals away from here before we leave," replied Sam as he drove the metal stakes into the ground and wrapped the blue and white tape around the entire riverbank area where the victim had been pulled ashore.

Cam nodded his approval and said, "Thank you Officer Parker, see you on the other side."

Sam just nodded and walked back towards the white van signaling for the team to climb back into the vehicle.

As Cam made his way back up the path to his patio overlooking the Wye, he was met by Helen coming out the kitchen door with a cup of tea in her hand.

"I saw you coming and figured you could use this. I laid out a fresh change of clothes on the bed for you. I knew you'd want to go right back to work," said Helen handing Cam the cup of steaming tea.

"Thanks darling," replied Cam as he turned to stare back down at the Wye. When he turned around, Helen had disappeared back into the house. All the years of marriage to Cam had taught her he didn't like any death which his instincts told him was the least bit suspicious. His gentle manner with the corpse also told Helen he was thinking of their own daughter and still grieving over their separation. When Cam was in one of what Helen could only describe as one of his 'black' moods she gave him time to himself.

Gazing in through the kitchen window, Cam watched as Helen hustled back and forth in the kitchen and smiled as he thought, 'she seems to anticipate my every need. It was my lucky day when I wandered into that book stall. She's one in a million.'

Draining the last of the warm, sweet tea from the cup, Cam wandered into the kitchen where Helen was washing dishes and leaned down and kissed the nape of her neck.

"Thanks. I'll try not to be too late. But until we confirm the cause of death, please lock up while I'm gone."

Helen turned to stare up into the grim face of her husband and asked, "Do you think she could've been murdered, Cam?"

"I don't know Helen, but I do know I don't want to leave anything to chance when it comes to you. So, please lockup tight."

Taking her husband's face in her hands, she kissed him and said, "I promise. Now go get that shower. You're dripping river water all over my clean floor!"

Within a half-hour, Cam had showered and was pressing the buzzer at the wrought iron entrance gate to Wilton Castle. Within minutes, a female voice answered, "May I help you?"

"Chief Inspector Fergus of West Mercia Police, I'd like to speak to Mrs. Parsons."

""Speaking, Chief Inspector. Mary Hamilton telephoned and said you would be dropping by. I'll buzz you in."

Within seconds, the gates swung open and Cam climbed back into his car and drove through. He had just exited his car, when he was greeted by Mrs. Parsons' black Labrador, Bella. Bending over to pet the friendly dog, Cam was reminded of his childhood pets and made a note to himself that now that he and Helen were settled it would be a perfect time to get a dog to share their love of walking around the Forest of Dean.

"I see you've met our Bella," said Mrs. Parsons as she approached across the gravel drive.

Rising to his feet, Cam smiled as he replied, "Yes ma'am. She's lovely. I've been thinking that now my wife and I are settled-in, it might be time to have a dog again. With the schedule I keep, he'd be company and protection for my wife, Helen."

Reaching down and lovingly stroking her pet, Mrs. Parsons replied, "Bella is a wonderful companion but not much of a guard dog these days, unless someone can be licked to death.

34

But you're not here to talk about dogs, so why don't we go inside and have a cup of coffee while you tell me what I can do to assist the West Mercia Police."

Entering through the front door, Cam felt like he had been transported back in time. As he followed, Mrs. Parsons through to the kitchen at the end of the hall, she stopped momentarily at the door to the dining room and pointed at a beautiful stained glass window.

"That window was the only remaining stained glass window from the original Elizabethan manor house. We were very fortunate to be able to have it restored to its original condition."

Cam was reminded of the magnificent stained glass windows of the castle back home in Scotland where he had given tours as a young man and remarked, "It is indeed beautiful. You are to be complemented on your restoration work here."

Mrs. Parsons smiled and said, "Thank you Chief Inspector. It's been a labor of love but bloody hard work."

Cam couldn't help but chuckle at hearing the word "bloody" escape the lips of such a refined lady.

Entering the kitchen, Cam again marveled at the sympathetic restoration work. Although, equipped with every modern day convenience it still maintained the charm of the original manor house.

Pointing at the farmhouse table, his hostess said, "Have a seat, Chief Inspector."

"This is a lovely room Mrs. Parsons. I see you've managed to retain some of the original features."

"We certainly have, Chief Inspector. Just behind you is actually the original Elizabethan manor house well," beamed Mrs. Parsons.

Looking around the warm and cozy kitchen, Cam watched as Bella made her way to her bed and circled twice before curling up close to where his mistress was preparing the coffee. On the other side of Bella's bed was another smaller bed with a ball of white fur curled up tight.

Carrying a tray laden with coffee, cream and sugar to the table, Mrs. Parsons noticed Cam's curious expression and smiled over at the sleeping cat and said, "That's our Miss Kitty. She used to be quite a mouser but now at twenty-one she only leaves her bed to eat or use her litter box."

Cam's mother always kept cats at the farm and knew the value of a good mouser but he had never heard of a cat living that long. It was a fine testimony to her owners' loving care of her.

"So, Chief Inspector, Mary said something about a drowning. How can I be of assistance?" asked Mrs. Parsons as she raised her coffee cup to her lips.

Taking a sip of coffee, Cam replied, "It would appear the body may have entered the river from this side and possibly from your estate. We'll need to do a search of the grounds. I'll see the men are very careful and do not disturb your gardens."

"Of course, Chief Inspector, my husband isn't home at the moment but I'll be glad to show you and your men around the grounds."

They had just finished their coffee when a buzzing sound announced the arrival of the SOCO team at the castle's entrance gate.

"That's probably the search team arriving," said Cam as he rose to his feet and headed back down the hall to the front door as Mrs. Parsons buzzed the gate open.

Standing in the gravel driveway, Cam waved his arms around like a traffic cop indicating where he wanted the van to park. He had promised this lady her gardens would not be damaged and he always kept his promises.

As the team piled out of the van, they were joined by Mrs. Parsons, who had slipped into her wellies preparing for walking the gardens, and Bella, who was already eagerly greeting the newcomers.

"Gentlemen, this is the owner, Mrs. Parsons. She has agreed to show us around the gardens. You are to be extremely careful and watch where she walks, as much as possible, so you don't disturb any of the plantings or landscaping. They have spent considerable time and money restoring these gardens and we don't want to damage anything."

"Yes sir," sounded the reply in unison.

As they walked around the side of the manor house, the largest of the 12th century remains came into view. Cam couldn't help but wonder how they managed to shore them up.

As Mrs. Parsons pointed to the first ruin, she said, "These ruins were in danger of collapsing and being lost but thanks to the National Trust and some artisans we were able to save them."

Cam was familiar with the restoration assistance furnished by the National Trust and also knew a lot of the Parsons' blood, sweat and money had gone into the saving of these ruins. It was obviously a labor of love.

Mrs. Parsons walked across the perfectly manicured lawns, closely followed by the team, pointing out the features of the castle ruins as she went.

"There's about two acres of gardens here and all this is surrounded by what is now a dry moat. Just to the other side of the moat is the

River Wye. Looking at the height and thickness of the remaining walls and its deep moat you can see this castle would have been quite the formidable fortress in the 12th century. If you notice, there is a dovecote here. This round tower was built in the late 1100's for the castle defenses as witnessed by the arrow slots and also for living quarters for the lord's guests. It was converted during the 1600's when the lord decided he didn't need it for defense."

"Thank you for showing us around Mrs. Parsons. Is there anywhere specifically off-limits to the men?" asked Cam.

"Except for the flower beds, Chief Inspector, they are free to do what they need to do," replied Mrs. Parsons as she made her way across the lawn to the kitchen door.

"Thank you, Mrs. Parsons. We'll be very careful," replied Sam Parker as he and his men moved off to begin their search.

Cam had started to move away with the men when Mrs. Parsons called from the open kitchen door, "Chief Inspector, have you seen Bella?"

"No ma'am. I thought she was in the house. I don't see her out here," replied Cam as he looked around the garden. It was then he heard the unmistakable sound of a deep Labrador bark coming from down near the river.

"She's down by the river, ma'am. I'll see to her for you," called Cam.

As Cam approached, he noticed Bella was acting strangely and sniffing the grassy area leading down to the water's edge.

"Come here girl," called Cam but Bella simply stood her ground and stared back at Cam.

Slowly approaching the area, Cam noticed the long grass leading down to the river had been flattened out as if something had been rolled down the hill. Realizing what he was looking at, Cam skirted the area and stooped down beside Bella.

"Good girl, Bella. I think you may have saved us a lot of time."

Cam quickly called the team to the area and pointed to the grassy embankment and said, "I think she may have gone in here."

Sam was first to reply, "Well-spotted, Chief. Looks like you saved us from a late shift tonight."

"You can thank Bella. She's the one who led me here. I wonder what else she could tell us if she could talk."

43

As the team was taping off the perimeter of the riverbank and Cam was taking Bella back to his mistress at the castle, Sam caught up to him and said, "Sir, if the girl went into the water there then she didn't walk in on her own accord."

"I know, Officer Parker. If that is, in fact, the entry point then her body was rolled down the incline and pushed in the river either when she was unconscious or already dead. I want a fingertip search of the immediate area and then fan out from there. I'll let Mrs. Parsons know we will be here for the foreseeable future."

"Yes sir," replied Officer Parker as he turned and went back to instruct his team.

Leading Bella by her collar, Cam turned as he reached the kitchen door and saw the crime tape was already in place and the men were on their knees crawling along side-by-side searching for any possible clues left at the scene.

Mrs. Parsons met Cam at the door and stepping outside onto the stone patio to let Bella into the kitchen said, "I see you've found something."

"Yes Ma'am. Actually, it was your Bella who found it. She wouldn't come when I called her so I walked down there and found where we believed the victim actually entered the river."

"How very strange, I keep the gate locked at all times so I wonder how the poor soul got onto the grounds," exclaimed Mrs. Parsons.

The same thing had already crossed Cam's mind as he said, "I'm afraid we'll have to close the entire estate and ask that no one other than the family be allowed on the grounds until we can determine the murder wasn't committed here. Unfortunately, we'll need access to the grounds until the investigation is over."

Mrs. Parsons' hand shot to her mouth as she exclaimed, "Murder! I was under the impression it was a suicide."

"I'm afraid I can't discuss the investigation with you but from what we see, it appears the victim may have been rolled down the grassy slope and then dragged into the river."

"Oh, how horrible! Do you think we are in any danger here, Chief Inspector?"

"No ma'am. But there will be officers posted inside your gate and around your grounds so you will be perfectly safe. If you have any questions or think of anything at all that may help us in our enquiries, please give us a call. Here's my card."

Chapter 5

Cam was parking his car at the station when Sergeant Roberts came running down the front steps.

"Sir, we've just received a missing person's report for a woman meeting the victim's description. The man filing the report is still in the lobby. Do you want to speak with him?"

Climbing out of his car, Cam said, "Yes, thanks Sergeant Roberts. Can you go ahead and setup an interview room. I'll speak to him in the lobby first."

Roberts turned on his heel and bounded back up the steps eager to make a good impression on Cam. He was studying for a promotion and knew a good word from the Chief Inspector wouldn't hurt when it came to his turn to move up in the ranks.

Entering the lobby, Cam was confronted by an agitated man speaking in a loud voice.to a rather stressed-out looking desk sergeant. Walking up beside the tall, slightly balding, theatrical-appearing man, Cam asked, "Sergeant, is there a problem here?"

The man turned on Cam and sneered, "I'm talking to the sergeant here. You'll have to wait your turn."

Cam smiled as the Desk Sergeant raised an eyebrow and lowered his gaze to the papers in front of him as Cam flashed his identification and said, "Chief Inspector Fergus. I understand you're here to report a missing person. Why don't you come with me and we'll find a more comfortable place to sit and I'll personally take your information. Sergeant Welch, could you bring some tea to Interview Room One?"

Cam's handling of the situation seemed to calm the man as he muttered a quiet thank you and followed Cam down the hallway.

Once they were seated, Cam took his notepad from his coat pocket and leaned back casually in his chair as he asked, "Your name, sir?"

"My name if Jeffrey Morris and I am the director of the Cotswold Shakespearean Touring Troupe. We travel around the country during the summer months putting on Shakespearean plays in outside venues."

Making note of the man's name, Cam asked, "I understand you came here today to report a missing person. Is this a relative of yours?"

"No, Alicia Martin is a member of our troupe. Actually, she is our lead female actor."

"And when was the last time you saw Miss Martin?"

49

"It was after the play at the Castle. We had all gone over to the hotel, virtually right next door, and had a few celebratory drinks and then we all said goodnight and went to our rooms. Alicia didn't show up for breakfast the next morning and when Kim, another of the troupe, went to check on her, her bed hadn't been slept in and her street clothes were still there."

"Street clothes?" asked Cam.

"Yes, it appears she went missing in her costume."

A knock on the door signaled the arrival of Sergeant Walsh delivering the tea. Passing a cup across the table to Morris, Cam continued, "Can you describe what she was wearing?"

"Yes, of course. She was playing Hermia. We were putting on a *Mid-Summer's Night Dream*, you see, so she was wearing a flowing white cotton dress."

50

"Mr. Morris, you mentioned you were performing at the castle, would that be Wilton Castle?"

"Yes, we have performed there the last three summers. We always have a good turnout. We are hoping to do *Romeo and Juliet* there in the future. The Parsons have completely restored the tower and it's an ideal set."

Cam nodded and quietly asked, "Mr. Morris, do you have Miss Martin's next of kin's details?"

Rubbing his chin, he replied, "Not with me. I'd have to phone the office and see if they can locate it. Why? What is it that you're not telling me, Inspector?"

"We pulled a young lady from the Wye this morning. We'd like to get a formal identification from the family to perhaps rule out or confirm the victim's identity," replied Cam gently.

"My God, you must be mistaken. It couldn't be Alicia. There's no way she'd commit suicide."

Cam stared across the table at the obviously shaken man and replied, "I don't believe I said anything about suicide, Mr. Morris. At the moment, we're still treating this as a suspicious death. But since you brought it up, what makes you think Miss Martin wouldn't consider taking her own life?"

"It just isn't possible, Inspector. She had a promising career, a supportive family and a loving fiancée. She had just accepted his marriage proposal last night. She'd have been the very last person who would ever walk into the river, considering her fear of water."

"She was afraid of water?" asked Cam.

"Yes, I remember that distinctly. Apparently, when she was a child she was playing near a river while on holiday with her family and slid down the bank and almost drowned. She even clinched her eyes shut whenever the tour bus went over a bridge."

"Mr. Morris, you mentioned a fiancée. Do you know how to locate him?"

"Of course, Chief Inspector, he's a member of our troupe. Alan plays Lysander, the lead male role opposite Alicia. He'd be at the hotel with the rest of the group. But now that you ask, I don't remember seeing him this morning."

Sliding the phone across the desk to Morris, Cam said, "If you'll call your office and get Miss Martin's family details, I'll send a car around to the hotel to pick up her fiancée. What is the young man's name?"

"Certainly, Inspector, his name is Alan Burke."

Cam pushed back from the table and rose to his feet and went to the front desk leaving Martin to make the call.

"Sergeant Walsh would you send one of the officers over to the hotel next to Wilton Castle and ask a young man name Alan Burke to accompany him here to the station?

"Yes sir. Roberts is still in the back finishing paperwork. I'll send him."

Cam nodded his approval and returned to the interview room where Morris was just hanging up the phone.

"I have the details for you but I'm afraid they won't do you any good. It seems they are on a tour of the States with no fixed itinerary."

"Alright, then we'll wait for the fiancée to arrive and take him over for the identification. I thank you very much for your co-operation Mr. Morris. We'll be in touch if we need any more information but for the time being, we don't want you or any of the troupe to leave town. Understood?"

Morris instantly began to sputter and stammer about their additional performances at other venues causing Cam to turn on him and sternly repeat, "You and your entire troupe are to remain in Ross until we advise you that you may leave. If the victim is Miss Martin, I'll need statements from all of you."

Cam followed Morris out the station as Sergeant Roberts was just coming through the door.

"He seems to have disappeared, Sir. No one in the troupe has seen him since last night either."

Morris suddenly stopped dead and turned on his heel with a relieved look on his face and said, "Oh thank goodness. They've probably gone off together. You know how young love can be, Chief Inspector."

"We'll still need to interview the rest of the troupe, Mr. Morris. We'll meet you there within the hour, if you can gather them together for us."

"Certainly, Chief Inspector, if you still think it's necessary."

"That I do," replied Cam as he noticed a flurry of activity at the station door.

As soon as Morris drove away, Sergeant Roberts joined Cam and said, "We've just had a 999 call from Father Michael at St. Mary's, he was closing up the church for the evening and discovered a body."

Nodding, Cam took off on foot running up the hill to the church right up from the station, leaving Sergeant Roberts to phone for SOCO and Mary Hamilton. The church sitting high on a hill with its spire towers rising 205 feet into the air was one of the most recognizable landmarks in Ross and could be seen for miles away. It was a church Cam knew well, as he and Helen attended services there on a regular basis. Rounding the bend into the churchyard, he was met by Father Michael, leaning heavily on the Plague Cross, which marked the graves of the three hundred or more townspeople who had been buried quickly at night during the plague outbreak of 1637.

Catching his breath from the uphill run, Cam put his arm around the aging man and gently asked, "Are you alright, Father Michael?"

Nodding slowly, he replied, "Yes, Chief Inspector. It's was only the shock of finding that young man, lying there like that. I thought I was seeing things at first. I truly did. You would think with all the burials I reside over the sight of a dead body wouldn't upset me but this is different."

Never having seen Father Michael behave anyway other than completely calm and in control of his feelings, Cam knew in an instant this wasn't just another dead body. Taking

Father Michael by his arm Cam asked, "Are you up to showing me where you found the body?"

"Yes, I'll be alright now. Just needed to get outside and get some fresh air. The shock, you understand."

Cam nodded as the two men made their way back up to the church as sirens rang out breaking the still evening air.

As they entered the dimly lit church and walked down the aisle, Father Michael pointed to his right toward the alcove immediately below the majestic stained glass window, where the members of the Ruddell family's monuments lie. Draped across the tomb-like burial monuments of the reclining Lord and Lady of Ruddell Manor, Cam could barely make out the body of what appeared to be a twenty-something-year-old male.

Seating Father Michael in the closest pew, Cam slipped into his gloves and carefully leaning over the body as not to disturb it before SOCO and Mary arrived, placed his gloved finger to the victim's throat checking for a pulse. There was none.

Chapter 6

Mary Hamilton was first to arrive at the church and called over to Cam as she came bustling down the center aisle, "I was having tea at your place with Helen when the call came in. What have we now, another suicide?"

Rubbing his brow, Cam shook his head and said, "I don't know about this one Mary, but I can almost guarantee you our victim from this morning didn't walk into the Wye on her own."

Mary raised her eyebrow, "You know something I don't then. The toxicology results won't be back until the end of the week at the earliest and there was no real trauma to the body except some scratches which would be consistent with her time in the water."

Cam said, "Yeah I know, but we discovered something this morning over at the Castle."

As Mary made her way around the body directing the newly arrived crime scene photographer, Cam waited patiently for her assessment of the scene and the victim.

"I'll need to get the body off of this crypt and onto the bag before I can tell you anything. Since you're gloved up, care to lend a hand Cam?"

"Sure Mary," replied Cam as he placed his arms under the young man's shoulders and on Mary's command helped move him to the waiting body bag laid out on the floor.

As Cam stood back, Mary began circling the victim like a predator circling its prey and scribbling notes. Cam enjoyed watching the woman do her work. Her job was unpleasant in Cam's view but no matter what the condition of the corpse, it was always treated with gentleness and dignity by Mary. She had a deep respect for the dead and an even deeper respect for the living they left behind to grieve them.

"Time of death, Mary?" asked Cam.

"I'd say it was about an hour later than the victim from this morning, so around midnight last night. But there's something unusual about this victim. Have a look around his mouth, Cam. What do you see?"

Squatting down next to Mary, Cam looked closely at the young man before looking over at Mary and asking, "What's that white residue around his lips?"

"Well Cam, my guess is he was frothing from the mouth before he died, could be any number of reasons for that."

Once finished with the preliminary examination, Mary reached into the victim's pants pocket and handed his wallet over to Cam. Flipping it open, he said solemnly, "Seems our victim is Alan Burke."

"You act like you recognize the name, Cam?"

Pulling a photo out of the wallet, Cam held it up for Mary to see. It was a picture of a smiling Alan Burke with his arms around the young girl they had pulled from the Wye earlier that day.

"Oh dear, do you think it was a murder/suicide?" asked Mary.

"Not sure yet Mary but evidence is pointing to the young lady not walking into the river on her own."

"Well, we'll know more when I get the autopsy done tomorrow," replied Mary as she motioned for her team to load up the body for the trip to the morgue.

As she turned to follow the body, she called back to Cam, "I'll have my preliminary report on both victims for you tomorrow. Give my love to Helen and try to get some rest."

As soon as Mary had moved away, Cam signaled for Sergeant Roberts to join him outside in the church yard. Looking around the church yard, Cam said' "We'll leave the team here to finish the search. We need to get over to the hotel and speak to Morris and the rest of the troupe."

The short drive across the Wye over the Wilton Bridge, which connected Ross-on-Wye to Wilton, only took minutes and Cam and Sergeant Roberts were soon hurrying in the front door of the hotel. Waiting in the bar area was a ruffled looking Morris and his troupe of young actors.

Rising to his feet, Morris said, "I hope you have good news for us and you've located our two young lovers and we can get on to our next venue."

Without replying, Cam walked to the bar and spoke quietly to the bartender before returning to the group and announcing, "I'll need to take statements from each of you separately in the private dining room. The rest of you are to wait in here until you're called."

"Is this really necessary, Chief Inspector? Surely, Alicia and Alan will turn up soon. They're probably on their way to our next stop in Chepstow as we speak."

"I'm very sorry to inform you that they have both turned up. We have two bodies awaiting formal identification in our morgue right now. Preliminary identification points to Miss Martin and Mr. Burke."

Pointing to the petite brunette who had immediately began loudly weeping, Cam said, "Miss, if you can compose yourself we'll speak with you first, if you'll follow me and the sergeant."

Sobbing into her handkerchief, the young woman followed Cam and Sergeant Roberts into the back room.

"Miss, may we have your name for the record?' asked Cam as he passed her a glass of water.

"Yes sir, my name is Kim Patrick. I play Helena."

"Well, Miss Patrick, can you tell us the last time you saw either Miss Martin or Mr. Burke?" asked Cam.

"It was after the play. We had all come back here to have a few drinks to celebrate and they walked down by the river. When I looked out the window, I saw them. They appeared to be having an argument."

"Could you hear what they were talking about?"

"No sir, I stayed inside. I could only see them from the window. I didn't want to intrude; besides they seemed to argue a lot so no one really paid much attention to it."

Cam walked over to the window and looked down towards the river bank and said, "Quite a distance from here and if you couldn't hear them, how can you be sure they were arguing?

"I saw Alan put his hands on Alicia's shoulders and she shoved him back and stormed off down the path in the direction of the castle."

"I see and what did Mr. Burke do?" probed Cam.

"Well, he stood there for a few minutes turned and started back to the hotel, and then turned back around and went off after her. I didn't see either of them again after that and now you're telling me they're both dead. Oh, I wish I'd gone after them. Do you know how they died?" asked the girl as she began sobbing heavily again into her handkerchief.

Helping Kim to her feet and walking her to the door Cam gently said, "I'm sorry miss but this is an ongoing investigation and I can't divulge any additional information. That will be all for now. No one will be allowed to leave town until the investigation is over but if you remember anything at all you can contact either Sergeant Roberts or me."

Leaving Kim to be consoled by Mr. Morris, Sergeant Roberts called the next member of the group.

Looking up from his notes as the nervous looking young man with long blond hair enter the room, Cam said, "Sit down son. I'm Chief Inspector Fergus. Can you tell us your name for the records?"

Sliding his long frame into the chair opposite Cam, the young man replied, "My name is Joseph Cotton. I play Demetrius in the play. I can't believe they're dead, Chief Inspector. Don't get me wrong, I was no big fan of Alan Burke. Frankly, I didn't like the way he treated Alicia and she just let him get away with it. She could have done so much better."

All his years of interviewing witnesses had left Cam with an amazing ability to read-between-the-lines and glean what a person was hinting at without actually saying.

Leaning back in his chair, Cam looked straight into the young man's eyes and asked, "So son, how long have you been in love with Miss Martin?"

Raising his head and pushing his hair back from his eyes, Cam watched as tears began to well up in the young man's blue eyes and roll down his hollow cheeks.

"Since we were in school, I really don't like this acting gig. I'm a musician and my dream is to play in a rock band. This was Alicia's dream and I just joined the troupe to be close to her. Kind of watch out for her, you understand. I always hoped she would finally see Alan for what he was and maybe then I would have a chance."

Handing the young man his handkerchief, Cam asked, "When was the last time you saw Miss Martin and Mr. Burke, Mr. Cotton?"

"Last night after the performance, they stayed behind in the garden and I went back to the hotel with the rest of the troupe."

Nodding Cam asked, "Where were you between the hours of 10pm and midnight?"

"I was in the bar for a while and then went up to my room. Why, you don't think I had anything to do with this, do you?" replied Cotton jumping to his feet.

"Sit down, please Mr. Cotton. We are asking everyone so we can eliminate them from our enquiries. Now were you alone?"

"Not in the bar, but I went to my room alone and went right to sleep. It had been a long day and we were supposed to have an early start this morning."

71

Cam nodded as he said, "Thank you for your cooperation, Mr. Cotton. That will be all for now. No one will be allowed to leave town until the investigation is over but if you remember anything at all you can contact either Sergeant Roberts or me."

For the better part of another hour, Cam and Sergeant Roberts continued to interview the rest of the troupe and take their statements before releasing them for the night after repeating their instructions to not leave the area. As they were leaving, Cam turned to Roberts and said, "Well Sergeant, they all claim to have been in their rooms alone, so not one alibi among the group except for Morris who was complaining to the manager about a noisy couple in the next room. It would appear we have a whole room of possible suspects, if this doesn't turn out to be a murder/suicide."

Yawning widely despite the volume of coffee he had consumed during the late night interviews, Cam continued, "I think we need to call it a night. It's been a very long day. Hopefully, we'll know more after Mary finishes the autopsies tomorrow and then we'll go from there. You take the car and get home to your family. I need a breath of fresh air so I'll walk home."

"Are you sure, sir? It's terribly late and you must be exhausted. I know I am," replied Sergeant Roberts as he stood looking down at the older man.

Placing his hands on the table, Cam slowly pushed himself up from the table and straightening up, patted his Sergeant on the back and smiled as he said, "Perfectly certain. It's a short walk over the bridge and up the hill to home, so it won't take me long."

As he crossed the bridge from Wilton to Ross, Cam stopped in the middle and watched as the light from the moon danced across the waters of the Wye and thought of the two young lovers whose futures had been so cruelly stolen from them.

Chapter 7

It was late afternoon the next day when Mary Hamilton phoned Cam with the autopsy results.

"Cam, it would appear your instincts were correct in this case," said Mary.

"So murder/suicide, as I suspected?" replied Cam as he started to scribble notes.

"Well, I can concur that Miss Martin was dead before she went in the water. No water in her lungs, you see, so she didn't drown. I'll have to wait on the toxicology report to determine cause of death since there are no signs of trauma on her body."

Cam sighed as he continued, "So it looks like Mr. Burke committed suicide after killing Miss Martin. What a bloody waste of two promising young lives."

"I'm not so sure he did, Cam," replied Mary.

"You're not sure if he killed her or if he committed suicide," asked Cam.

"Neither Cam, you see once I got him on the slab, I found bruising indicating Mr. Burke had been restrained before death and all my instincts lead me to believe someone may have either drugged him or poisoned him. I have put a rush on the toxicology reports for both victims. I think we have a murderer on the loose, Cam."

Exhaling deeply into the phone, Cam replied, "Thanks Mary, please call me the minute you hear back from them."

"Will do, Cam and be careful."

Hanging up the phone, Cam walked to the white board in the incident room and began scribbling names under the photos of the victims. Cam was standing there scratching his head as Sergeant Roberts returned from picking up their lunch.

"Sir? What's going on?" asked Sergeant Roberts as he set the tea down and moved to stand beside his commander at the board.

"According to the autopsy, we may have a double murder on our hands. Mary has determined Miss Martin was dead before she went into the Wye and Mr. Burke had bruising indicative of being bound. If this is correct, then we have a murderer on the loose. We'll know more when the toxicology reports come back. I think Mary is assuming some type of poison or other drug may be involved."

"Where do we go from here, Chief Inspector?" asked Roberts.

"I don't think these are random murders committed by a stranger and since the victims are not known by anyone local I think we need to concentrate on their fellow actors. Do you agree?" asked Cam looking over at his young Sergeant.

"I do, sir. May I suggest putting a cat among the pigeons?"

"You're suggesting putting an undercover officer at the hotel, Sergeant Roberts?" asked Cam.

"Yes sir. I think we've already eliminated Mr. Morris from our enquiries, so if you trust him then we could plant PC Anne Parks with the group as a potential replacement for Miss Martin. She's been active in amateur theater, so she shouldn't raise suspicion."

"I don't believe I've met her, but surely one of the locals will recognize her and blow her cover."

Smiling brightly Sergeant Roberts replied, "That's the beauty of it, sir. Today is her first day reporting for duty. She's a transfer from York and hasn't even had time to find accommodations yet, so no one in town has met her. She's in the cafeteria, shall I bring her in?"

"Yes, bring her in, and Sergeant, well done, excellent idea."

Within minutes, Sergeant Roberts was back followed by a thin, jean-clad, raven-haired woman in her twenties. Stepping into the room, the young lady extended her hand to Cam and gripping it strongly said, "Nice to meet you, Chief Inspector Fergus."

"Welcome aboard, PC Parks. Have a seat and we'll brief you on the investigation," replied Cam.

Moving back to the whiteboard, Cam pointed to the photographs of the two young victims and continued, "The first victim was Alicia Martin. Her body was recovered from the River Wye yesterday morning. Later in the day, Alan Burke's body was found draped across a crypt in St. Mary's Church, just up the hill from here. Mr. Burke was Miss Martin's fiancé."

Cam hesitated at this point to see if PC Parks was going to draw any conclusions from the amount of information he had divulged, but she sat stoically still waiting for him to continue.

"We are still awaiting toxicology results but the autopsy results indicate despite giving the initial appearance of a murder/suicide that both the victims were murdered."

Standing up and joining Cam at the board, PC Parks pointed to the names of the acting group and asked, "I take it these are your suspects? So, if you are right, then one or more of them murdered this couple and tried to make it appear as a murder/suicide. What can I do to help Chief Inspector?"

"Sergeant Roberts tells me you have acting experience and since you are new to the area and not known to locals, we'd like you to join with the acting troupe as a replacement for Miss Martin and see what inside information you can get from them. We have already eliminated the director of the group, Mr. Morris, and we'll need to have him in on the mission. I'm not anticipating any problem with him agreeing since he wants to get this wrapped up so they can get on with their tour."

"What play are they putting on, Chief Inspector?" asked PC Parks.

This time it was Roberts that responded, "They're doing *Mid-Summer's Night Dream*, Anne."

"Good, I have played both Hermia and Helena, so I already know the lines."

"Well good. Let's get Morris over here and fill him in. Sergeant, will you go over and bring him in. You can tell him that in lieu of available next of kin, we'll need him to confirm the identities of the deceased. That shouldn't raise suspicion."

Once Roberts had left, Cam turned his attention to his new PC and asked, "How about some coffee while we discuss the logistics."

"Yes sir," replied Anne as she walked through the door Cam held open for her. As they walked down the hall to the small cafeteria, Anne asked, "How am I to get any information back to you sir?"

"I'll give you my mobile number and you're to program it into your phone using mum as the contact name, in the event that anyone picks up your phone. For the sake of your cover story, you have been living with you mother and father in York and are traveling during a break from your work with the local theater group. As soon as you hear anything that you think is relevant, call me, no matter what the time of day and if you feel in danger at any time, call for backup, understood? Remember, one or more of these people may have murdered two people already and they won't hesitate to make it three."

By the time, Cam and Anne had finished their coffee they were joined by Sergeant Roberts informing them that Mr. Morris was waiting in Interview Room One.

When they entered the room minutes later, Morris was white as a sheet and sweating profusely despite the coolness of the day.

Sitting down opposite him, Cam turned to Sergeant Roberts and said, "Would you bring Mr. Morris some water, Sergeant?"

Wiping the dripping sweat from his face, Morris suddenly blurted out, "Is this really necessary Chief Inspector? I've never seen someone who's been murdered before especially someone I was close to like these two young people."

"I must apologize, Mr. Morris; we have brought you here under false pretenses. We have already formally identified both victims. We have asked you here because we need your assistance in solving these crimes."

Morris continued to sweat but asked, "How can I be of assistance, Chief Inspector?"

Nodding in the direction of PC Parks, Cam replied, "This is PC Anne Parks and we'd like her to join your group. She is new in town so she won't be recognized by any locals and has actually performed in the same role as the deceased."

"So, if I understand you correctly Chief Inspector, then you believe that Alicia and Alan were killed by one of my group."

"We are not ruling out anyone at this point, with the exception of you. I would like to be able to eliminate the troupe from the investigation so that you can get on with your tour and since none of them have alibis then having PC Parks working undercover could expedite the process."

"I can't believe that one of my troupe would do anything so horrible but I'm willing to try anything that will get us on with the tour, Chief Inspector."

"Alright, we'll arrange for Anne to check into the hotel later today. What time do you usually all get together for dinner?" asked Cam.

"We normally eat in the pub area around 7pm."

Turning to face Anne, Cam continued, "Anne will be sitting at the bar before you get there. When you go up to order, she'll strike up a conversation with you during which you'll mention that you are dining with your theatrical group. At that point, she'll tell you that she is an actor and you'll invite her over to join your group. You can follow Anne's lead from there and end up inviting her to join the troupe for the balance of the tour. You think you can handle this PC Parks?"

"Yes sir."

"Any questions or concerns, Mr. Morris?"

"No, Chief Inspector. I used to be quite a good actor in my day so I shouldn't have a problem convincing them. I hope your plan works and it doesn't end up being one of my troupe."

Cam rose to his feet and extended his hand to Morris and as he shook hands he said, "Thank you so much for your co-operation. I hope we are wrong too."

Cam escorted Morris out to the lobby where Sergeant Roberts waited to drive him back to his hotel in Wilton and then returned to finish briefing PC Parks.

"Out of the group Chief Inspector, is there any one suspect that sticks out in your mind?" asked PC Parks.

86

Flipping through his interview notes, he pulls the file on the young actor playing Demetrius.

"There is one that stands out. His name is Joseph Cotton and he's playing Demetrius. Seems he'd been carrying a torch for Miss Martin and only joined the troupe to be near her. He freely admitted to not liking Mr. Burke and that could implicate him in his death, but to be honest, I can't see him hurting Miss Martin. He seemed genuinely crushed by her death."

PC Parks hesitated a moment before replying, "Well, he is an actor, sir. Maybe he just snapped and decided that if he couldn't have her then no one could."

"It's a possibility. In the meantime, try to get close to the entire group and see if you can pick up any gossip and get back to me as soon as you have any updates."

Chapter 8

As soon as Cam had pointed PC Parks in the direction of the hotel in Wilton, he headed home for dinner. As he turned down the street to home he noticed Mary's ancient Land Rover parked at the curb.

Turning the corner, he found Helen and Mary relaxing on the patio enjoying a pitcher of Pimms and catching up on town gossip.

Helen was the first to spot his approach and called out, "Care for a cool drink?"

"Yes, thanks Helen," replied Cam as he dropped into a chair sitting opposite Mary.

"How are you Mary? Keeping busy?" asked Cam.

"Yes sir. When I'm not working, the animals keep me busy. I had to come into Ross to get some groceries and feed and decided to drop in and bring Helen her eggs for the week and get a piece of her delicious Victoria Sponge, of course."

Just then Helen came out carrying the cake and an extra glass for Cam before heading back into the kitchen for plates and cutlery. While she was gone, Mary asked, "Any new developments in the case, Cam?"

"Not really Mary. It's early days yet," replied Cam as he poured his drink.

"The only one in the troupe that we can eliminate from the list of suspects is Mr. Morris. It seems that during the time frame that you gave us for the two deaths he was complaining vigorously to the landlord about being woken by some people partying in the room next door to his."

Thinking for a minute, Mary said, "Anyone could have rolled Miss Martin into the river; but I think it would take someone a lot stronger to overpower Mr. Burke and then get him to the church and position his body like that. So I'm thinking a man or perhaps even two people working together. Seems like with no alibis, the rest of the troupe would have opportunity but what about motive?"

"That's exactly what I'm trying to figure out. Perhaps jealousy, Mr. Cotton admitted his dislike for Burke and his affection for Miss Martin and he's a strapping young man and could easily have overcome the smaller Mr. Burke. Another scenario I've thought of is that Burke murdered his fiancée and Cotton witnessed it and murdered Burke. One of the female troupe members said she had seen Mr. Burke and Miss Martin arguing before they both disappeared."

As soon as Helen returned Mary quickly changed the subject to the upcoming August carnival.

"Every year the annual procession makes its way around the town's centre, showing off a fantastic display of floats and fancy dress. The parade ends at the Ropewalk where there's plenty of great entertainment including a fun fair, lots of stalls and all manner of food and drink. It's a great day out and well-attended."

Settling back down in her chair, Helen said, "Sounds like a nice day out and a much needed break from events of late."

Scraping the last bit of cake crumbs from her plate, Mary sighed and said, "Simply delicious, as always. I hate to leave such charming company but I need to get home and feed the animals and I'm sure your dinner is about ready."

Winking at Cam, Mary continued, "Helen was just popping a fish pie in the oven when I arrived. I understand that's your favourite."

Standing and walking Mary to her car, Cam replied, "That it is and Helen makes the best! Drive carefully and I'll speak with you tomorrow."

Waving out the window, Mary yelled, "Good night Helen! I'll stop by the station tomorrow, Cam. Enjoy your dinner."

It was just going on 11pm when PC Parks reported in for the first time. Cam could hear the background noise and knew Anne was calling from the hotel pub.

"Hi Mum, yes I'm fine. How are you? Great! I have some news for you and Dad. I've been invited to join the Cotswold Shakespearian Traveling Theatre group for the rest of their tour. Sorry Mum, I can't hear you. It's a bit noisy in here. Hang on a minute. Oye Kim, Mum can't hear me. I'm going to step out back for a while. See you later in our room."

Cam waited until the background noise disappeared and asked, "Everything OK, Anne?"

"Yes sir, Morris is quite a good actor. He had no trouble getting them to accept me. They have me rooming with Kim so we can practice our lines. She plays Helena. I met Joe Cotton and he seems genuinely upset. He told Mr. Morris tonight after dinner that he plans on leaving the troupe now that Alicia is gone. I think by Morris bringing me on so soon after Alicia's death that Joe felt like Morris only cared about the bottom line and not about the actors and their feelings. Joe more or less told him so, in not so many words, in front of the entire troupe at dinner. I don't mind telling you that I could tell Morris was pissed. He put on a good act telling Cotton how he understood completely, but I got the feeling that he is definitely one of those 'the show must go on' types. I'm taking a bottle of wine up to the room and see if I can get Kim to loosen up and find out the inner workings of the group. Hopefully, I'll have more concrete information for you tomorrow."

"Good work, Anne. Please remember, don't take any unnecessary chances. Call for backup if you feel the least bit threatened."

"Yes Mum, understood. I'll phone you again tomorrow, if I get a chance. Good night." Cam hung up the phone and tried to 'turn off his brain' and get some sleep but sleep wouldn't come.

Cam was still groggy the next morning and for the first time in years Helen had to wake him. Coming into the bedroom, Helen placed a cup of hot, strong coffee on the night stand before pulling open the curtains, letting the bright August sun stream in through the large sash windows.

"What time is it?" asked Cam as he struggled to sit up on the side of the bed.

"Almost time for you to leave for work. Breakfast will be ready in 10 minutes so you've got time for a quick shower."

"I don't think I'll have time for breakfast this morning."

Heading back into the kitchen, Helen called back over her shoulder, "Sergeant Roberts phoned and said he'll be around in a half hour to pick you up in the car, so you'll have time to eat."

"I was planning on walking to the station as usual. Did he say why he was picking me up?" asked Cam as he padded to the kitchen door before heading into the bathroom.

"He said he'd received a phone call last night and wanted to fill you in on the details in person."

"Well, he could have waited until I got to the station," mumbled Cam. Cam was a creature of habit and hated having his daily routine interrupted.

Cam was finishing his breakfast when Sergeant Roberts knocked on his back door.

"Come in, Roberts," called Cam as he got up from the table and went to the kitchen cabinet for another cup.

"Sit down Sergeant and have a cup of coffee while you tell me about this phone call."

Taking off his hat and sitting down opposite Cam, he waited until Helen filled his cup and left the room leaving the men to discuss police business in private.

"It was from Kim Patrick. You remember, she was the weepy one. The first one we took a statement from."

"Yes, Sergeant, I remember. What did she have to say?"

"It seems that she is convinced that Joseph Cotton murdered Alan Burke out of jealousy and said that there had been bad blood between them for weeks. Apparently, Miss Martin showed up one morning for breakfast a couple weeks back with a black eye and a bruise on her arm. She claimed that she fell but Kim had heard the couple arguing the night before and had mentioned it at the table before Miss Martin showed up. According to Miss Patrick, Mr. Cotton went after Mr. Burke and threatened to kill him if he ever hurt Miss Martin again. Apparently, a fight ensued and the police were called."

"Did she say exactly when and where they were performing at the time? We'll need to get the police report."

"Yes sir, already taken care of. That's why I told Mrs. Fergus I'd pick you up in a half hour. I was having the report faxed over to me. I even had time to speak to the officer who went out on the call."

"Well done, Sergeant. Let's have a look at it," said Cam.

As Cam waited for his sergeant to finish his coffee a call came through on his mobile. It was PC Parks checking in.

"Hello Anne. We were just heading over to the hotel to bring Mr. Cotton in for questioning. Seems Miss Patrick phoned Sergeant Roberts last night to let him know that Cotton had threatened Burke's life not long ago. The police were called to break up the fight. The report was faxed over to us this morning."

"Kim called, huh? Well, I overheard her tell Joseph that she'd get even with him," replied Anne.

"Get even?" asked Cam.

"Yeah, it seems that little Miss Kim is not the sweet, grieving friend of Alicia's that everyone thought. Apparently, she's been in love with Joseph Cotton all this time and jealous of Alicia because he was in love with her. Last night, Joseph had too much to drink and broke down grieving for Alicia. Kim started hanging all over him and told him that she was there for him and then told him that Alicia never cared about him and thought he was a joke."

"What happened next?" asked Cam.

"Well, Joseph shoved her away from him and called her a liar and told her she didn't know anything. Then he told her that she would be the last person on earth that he would be interested in. That was when Kim threw her drink in his face and he stormed out. I went after him, but he seems to have disappeared."

"Good work Anne. I'm glad you called when you did. We were just coming over to bring Mr. Cotton in for further questioning. We'll be over there shortly and for God's sake be careful."

Clearing her throat as a signal that someone was within hearing distance, Anne replied, "OK Mum, will do. Speak to you soon."

Hanging up the phone, Cam turned to his sergeant and said, "This case gets more bizarre every day."

"What did PC Parks have to say?" asked Sergeant Roberts.

"Well, it seems that we have any number of love triangles going on here. It seems that Kim has been carrying a torch for Joseph and let him know in no uncertain terms last night and he rejected her. She threatened to get even with him and threw her drink in his face. He stormed out and Anne went after him but couldn't find him."

"So, that's what you think prompted her call last night, huh?" asked Roberts.

"Sounds like it, Sergeant. Let's get over there and see if we can locate Mr. Cotton and have a word with little Miss Kim about wasting police time."

Pulling into the parking lot, Sergeant Roberts pointed in the direction of the riverbank and said, "I believe that's Miss Patrick over there."

"You go inside and see if Mr. Cotton is about. I'll go have a word with Miss Patrick," said Cam.

Cam found Miss Patrick weeping as she paced back and forth along the riverbank. As soon as she saw Cam approaching she ran to him saying, "I know he's done himself harm. I really upset him last night. We argued then I called the station and said those horrible things about him and now he's disappeared. I'm afraid he's thrown himself into the river and it's all my fault," she wailed.

"Calm down, Miss Patrick. What makes you think he's thrown himself into the river?"

"Well, right before we argued he was drinking heavily and said that he wished he was with Alicia. I tried to comfort him and I told him how I felt about him and that I was still here for him and he went off on me. I actually threw my drink in his face and he stormed out of the pub.

I'm so ashamed. Anne Parks, the new member of the group, went after him but she couldn't find him. I just know he's dead!" she cried.

"Let's get you inside, Miss Patrick and get you settled then Sergeant Roberts and I will attempt to locate Mr. Cotton. If you'll introduce me to Miss Parks then we'll start with her."

Putting his arm around the shaking shoulders of the still weeping Kim, Cam propelled her towards the pub where the rest of the troupe was sitting around the dimly lit room talking with Sergeant Roberts.

As soon as Cam entered the room with Kim, Anne came to meet them and took Kim in her arms and patting her on the back winked at Cam as she said to Kim, "I'm sure he's only gone off to sulk and sleep off last night's drink. Try not to worry Kim. You know how guys can be."

Breaking away from the hug and walking over to a table in the corner and dropping down onto the chair, Kim said, "That's what the Chief Inspector seems to think too but I just know something is wrong. I told him that you saw everything and went looking for Joseph so he wants to ask you some questions too, Anne."

Smiling up at Cam, Anne pushed open the door to the garden and asked, "Can you ask your questions outside, Chief Inspector? It's been a really nerve racking day and I rather fancy a cigarette, if you don't mind."

"Certainly, Miss Parks, I think we can accommodate that. Sergeant Roberts, will you take statements from Mr. Morris and the rest of the group while I speak to Miss Parks outside so she can have a cigarette?" asked Cam as he followed Anne out the door.

As soon as they were a sufficient distance from the pub, Anne said, "I really hope Kim is wrong

105

but to be honest I'm concerned for Joseph's welfare too. Mr. Morris and I went after him last night. I finally gave up after an hour but poor Morris was out until the wee hours looking for him. Poor old soul tripped and fell coming back up the path and made a hell of a mess of his hands. I offered to bandage them up for him but he went right up to his room. He was really worried about Joseph despite their argument about him leaving the troupe."

"I'm sure he feels responsible for these young people that he has had under his wing all summer. It can't be an easy job keeping all these young people in line and focused on their performances, especially with all the personal relationships going on. It's like a soap opera."

"Yeah, it must be stressful. Mr. Morris was just saying the other night that sometimes he misses his old gardening job. Quite a change in professions, huh?" asked Anne.

106

"Yeah, I figured he was a professor of English Literature since he was leading a Shakespearean acting troupe," replied Cam almost absentmindedly.

"Oh, when I said gardening, I didn't mean to imply that he wasn't a professor. Actually he is, but not of English Literature. He's a professor of botany. We had quite a lively conversation about different species of local plant life last night before the fracas started," replied Anne.

Just as Anne was putting out her cigarette, Sergeant Roberts popped his head out and called over, "I've finished taking the statements, sir."

"Thanks Sergeant, I'm finished with Miss Parks too so we can get a team over here to search the area. In the meantime, I want to see Mr. Cotton's room."

Ushering Anne back into the pub, Cam quickly approached Morris and asked, "Has anyone checked Mr. Cotton's room?"

"Yes, Chief Inspector. Kim and I went there first thing this morning, hoping to find him there sleeping it off but it doesn't appear that his bed was slept in."

"Well, I'd like to see his room, if you wouldn't mind showing me the way," replied Cam.

"Certainly," replied Morris as he made his way out of the pub and into the hotel lobby and up the stairs to the rooms above.

As the two men approached the door to Mr. Cotton's room, Cam reached into his pocket and pulled on the latex crime scene gloves. As Morris paced up and down outside the door in the hallway, Cam began his methodical search of the room. Finding all the dresser drawers empty, he moved onto the suitcase lying open

108

on the bed. Pushing all of the clothing aside, Cam's fingers close around a glass vial. Pulling it out and walking to the door, Cam held up the vial and asked, "Mr. Morris, to the best of your knowledge did Mr. Cotton have a drug problem?"

Staring at the vial, Morris replied "Not that I'm aware of Chief Inspector, but the rest of the group may know more about his personal habits. It really isn't something that he would admit to me, being his employer."

"I understand Mr. Morris. Let's go back downstairs and see what they have to say about it."

Kim was the first one Cam approached. Holding up the vial, he asked, "Kim, have you ever seen this before?"

"No sir, what is it?" she asked.

"That's what I'm trying to find out," replied Cam as he walked around the room, holding the vial up for the rest of the assembled group to see.

"Have any of you ever seen this vial before or have any idea what this powder is inside it?" Cam continued.

Cam's question was met with a shaking of heads and silence. Growing impatient to what Cam felt was the closing of ranks among the troupe he finally declared, "Look, I'm not accusing any of you of possession of illegal drugs, I'm just trying to ascertain if any of you might have had any knowledge of or suspicion that Joseph may have been using drugs of any sort."

That seemed to break the ice as Kim quietly said, "I've known him to smoke a little weed now and then but never anything heavy. I've never seen him with that vial. Are you sure it's his?"

"It would appear to be, since I found it in his suitcase."

The slamming of the pub door announced the return of Sergeant Roberts from leading the search team.

"Anything, Sergeant?" asked Cam.

"Nothing in the immediate area, should I have team fan out downstream?"

Cam had no sooner nodded his head as a sign of approval then Kim began wailing and screaming hysterically, "I knew he's thrown himself in the river and it's all my fault!"

One look from Cam to Anne sent the young PC quickly moving to Kim's side and wrapping her arms around her to try to calm her.

As soon as Kim was calmed down, Cam continued, "We are not taking anything for granted and we'll be checking the entire area for Mr. Cotton. At this point in the investigation, we're just considering this as a missing person incident. Normally, we wouldn't even looking into his disappearance so soon; however, because he is in a fragile state due to the recent deaths, we will give this our full attention. As soon as we have any information, we'll keep you informed and if any of you think of anything that could possibly aid us in this investigation we ask that you contact us immediately."

Turning on his heel, Cam headed out the door towards Sergeant Roberts and his awaiting car. Before he could get in the car, Anne appeared at the door lighting a cigarette and signalling with her head that she wanted to speak with him. Making her way up the narrow country lane towards the main road, Anne waited until Cam's car approached.

Rolling the window down, Cam asked, "You got something for me?"

"Just a thought, Joseph always left his door unlocked so anyone could have placed that vial in there."

"OK, thanks Anne. Good work," replied Cam.

Stomping out her cigarette, Anne turned and walked back to the hotel pub to join the rest of the group. As she entered the hotel, Morris was waiting and said, "Rehearsal in ten minutes in the back garden. I came looking for you and saw the Chief Inspector talking to you. Is everything alright?"

"Yeah, thanks Mr. Morris, he just wanted to thank me for calming down Kim. Apparently, the Chief Inspector doesn't deal well with hysterical females," replied Anne as she entered the hotel and smiled at what she could only describe as protective, doting-father behaviour.

Chapter 9

It was around noon on Thursday when Mrs. Parsons rang the station and asked for Cam.

"Hello, Chief Inspector. Mrs. Parsons here, I have a favor to ask of you."

"Yes, Mrs. Parsons. What can I do for you?"

"I know you asked that we not leave the area but I was wondering if it would be alright for me to leave for the day and drive down to visit my daughter. She and her family normally come here for the weekends but with so much happening here I didn't think it would be a good idea to have the grandchildren running all over your crime scene. My husband will, of course, be going with me but Bella will be home guarding the house," she chuckled at the thought of the overly friendly, aging Labrador scaring away an intruder.

Cam genuinely liked the gracious lady of the manor and replied "I am sure that will be just fine, Mrs. Parsons. We deeply regret any inconvenience this has caused you."

"Oh, think nothing of it, Chief Inspector. Only too happy to cooperate with the police and it was lovely meeting you. Perhaps when this is all over, you'll bring your wife to see the gardens."

"Thank you, Mrs. Parsons. I'm sure Helen would enjoy that very much. We're directly across the river from you and she often admires the ruins from our patio. Enjoy your day out with your family and we'll be in touch."

On Thursday evening when Mr. and Mrs. Parsons returned from their day out, Bella was sitting inside the front gate waiting for them.

"Something's wrong. I know Bella was in her bed in the kitchen when I locked up the house before we left. I'm phoning the police. We'll wait for here in the car for them to arrive," said

Mr. Parsons as he reached for his mobile and quickly dialed 999.

Within minutes, sirens announced the arrival of the police followed immediately by Cam and Sergeant Roberts. As soon as Mr. Parsons explained his concerns, Cam left an officer with the Parsons in the drive as he and Sergeant Roberts entered the house. Nothing seemed to be disturbed until they reached the kitchen,

"Here's where they gained entry," said Cam as he pointed to a broken pane of glass in the kitchen door.

"Looks like someone was in a hurry to get out of here," noted Sergeant Roberts as he looked around at the kitchen chairs lying around the room on their sides.

Suddenly remembering the other member of the Parson household, Cam walked over and reached down and stroked the head of Miss

117

Kitty. A soft purr assured Cam that she had not been harmed by the intruders.

"Sergeant, would you go out and ask the Parsons to come in now. They'll need to have a look around to see what, if anything is missing. Please ask them not to touch anything. We'll want to dust for fingerprints."

Nodding, Roberts soon returned with the distressed couple. After a complete search of the manor house the only thing they could find missing was some loose change that Mr. Parsons had emptied from his pockets and left in a dish by the front door the evening before.

"From the looks of what they took, I'm thinking that it might have been juveniles, but we'll have SOCO dust for prints. Hopefully, if it's not youngsters the prints will match with someone in our files and we can get them off the streets. I'm glad they didn't do any damage in the house or hurt Bella or Miss Kitty."

A scratching at the back door announced the arrival of Bella. Opening the door wide, Mr. Parsons let her in, but instead of going to her favorite spot on her bed, she clamored under the table and began scratching at the cover of the old well and whining.

"Come away Bella, you silly girl," called Mrs. Parsons before Cam held up his hand and in a hushed voice said, "Did you hear that?"

"I sure did. Sounds like something is bumping against the side of the old well," replied Mr. Parsons as he gently moved Bella away from the well so he could examine it more closely.

"Chief Inspector, this cover's been taken off. Wc had it sealed for safety reasons during the renovations. Help me get this cover off!"

Cam griped a hold of one side of the cover and the two men lifted the cover off the deep, dark well.

Retrieving a torch from the drawer by the door, Mr. Parsons switched it on and peered down into the well.

"Oh my God," uttered Mr. Parsons.

Calmly, Cam turned to Mr. Parsons and said, "Perhaps it would be better if you take your wife out of the kitchen while I call for help and ask Sergeant Roberts to come in. He's at the gate waiting for SOCO to arrive."

"Certainly, Chief Inspector," replied Mr. Parsons as he lead his wife out of the kitchen speaking with her in hushed tones.

Cam quickly dialed the station, "Sergeant Walsh, can you get the Fire Brigade over to Wilton Castle. We have a body down the well and we'll need their help extraditing it."

Cam had just hung up as Sergeant Roberts came running into the kitchen.

"SOCO just arrived and Mr. Parsons said there's another body."

Shining the torch back down into the well, Cam waited as Roberts' mind registered what he was looking at, "Looks like someone pushed him in head first. How are we going to get him out?

"The Fire Brigade is on the way and they'll have the necessary equipment. Can you call Mary and let her know where we are and that we have another body for her."

"Who do you think it is?" asked Roberts as he was dialing Mary Hamilton.

"The only thing I can say for certain is that the victim is male based on his foot size. But I have a bad feeling that it might be our missing Joseph Cotton. We'll know for sure when we get him out of there. Stay here, while I speak to SOCO and let them know we have another murder scene and not just a burglary, as we thought."

Before he could reach the front door, Mr. Parsons stopped Cam and asked, "Chief Inspector would it be alright if I took my wife back down to stay with our daughter tonight? This has upset her greatly. I'll drive straight back and stay here overnight with Bella, of course. Don't want to leave the house unattended again."

"Of course, Mr. Parsons, I think that's an excellent idea and I'm terribly sorry that this has happened in your home," replied Cam as he reached over and patted the older gentleman on his shoulder.

As Mrs. Parsons was packing her overnight bag for the return to her daughter's the fire brigade arrived. Meeting the brigade chief in the drive, Cam said, "Mrs. Parsons has been understandably upset by this evenings discovery so if you don't mind waiting to remove the body until she and her husband leave I'll show you where he is."

Stretching his hand out to Cam the brigade chief said, "I don't believe we've met, Chief Inspector. I'm the chief in charge, Keith Bilhams. I know the owners and I can quite understand so no problem waiting."

"Thanks for understanding, Chief Bilhams. I'm Cam Fergus. I haven't been assigned here very long so we haven't had the opportunity to meet. Sorry to have to meet under these circumstances. It seems like we're having quite a crime spree this week."

"Really, Chief Inspector I hadn't heard. This is the first call out we've had for rescue," replied Chief Bilhams as he followed Cam down the hall to the kitchen.

"The other two victims, unfortunately, didn't require rescue. They were already deceased by the time they were discovered. I actually pulled the first victim out of the Wye myself and Father Michael found the second victim in the church," said Cam.

Shining the torch down the well, Cam waited while Chief Bilhams accessed the situation. The well was deep and relatively narrow and the victim appeared to be tightly wedged. After one final look, he turned to Cam and said, "I'm pretty sure he's wedged tight so trying to pull him out by his feet isn't likely to work. We'll give it a try first but I have a feeling that someone is going to have to be lowered down there to place a harness around the body. We've done well rescues before but in almost all those cases they were for animals."

Just then, Mr. Parsons stuck his head in the door and said, "Hi Keith, I see the Chief Inspector called you out. Thanks for coming so quickly. I'm off to drop the Missus down to the daughters for the night. I'll be back in a few hours."

"Take your time, Mr. Parsons. We should have the crime scene cleaned up by the time you return. Don't worry about your house. I'll have officers stationed at the front and back for the rest of the night," replied Cam.

As soon as the Parsons had left, Chief Bilhams made his way outside to his crew waiting patiently by the truck and returned with a hoist and two of his larger crew members.

Slipping the rope down the well, Bilhams managed to loop it around the victim's feet on the first try and looking over at Cam said, "We'll give it a go, but I'm not very optimistic. I think he's wedged in too tightly. Alright lads, on three, pull slowly."

The three men maneuvered around the outside of the well and pulled from every possible angle trying to shift the victim but to no avail.

Cam watched as Chief Bilhams stripped off his jacket and shirt and said, "Looks like I'm the smallest one here, so I'll be going down to fasten this around his midsection and try to move his body enough to loosen him."

Slipping into the safety harness, the chief called to his men, as he was lowered headfirst down into the well, "Slow and easy men. Let's get me and the victim out of here in one piece."

The Chief's legs had barely disappeared down the well when Mary came bustling into the already crowded kitchen.

Looking around the kitchen at what was going on she nodded at Cam and began to recite in a sing-song voice "Ding dong bell, a victim in the well. Who put him in there? That's for us to tell."

While the two firemen snickered, Cam shook his head disapprovingly and said, "Bad Mary…really bad."

126

Mary just grunted and reached over and tapped Chief Bilhams on the only part of his body protruding from the well, his feet, then leaned over and hollered down the well, "Get a move on Keith, I've got a dinner date tonight and need to get home in time to make myself beautiful."

"You're in rare form today, Mary. Any news on those toxicology results yet?" asked Cam.

"I phoned the lab earlier today and they assured me that they were almost finished and hope to be able to fax them to me by tomorrow morning at the latest."

"Alright lads, you can pull me up now," called the Chief.

Once Chief Bilhams was pulled out and helped to an upright position, he winked at Mary and said, "Pardon my appearance Mary but if you'll give us some room, we'll have the victim out in a jiffy. Alright men, easy does it, on my count of three."

Within minutes the body started to slowly rise from the well and before long was stretched out face-down on the stone kitchen floor.

Mary slipped into her crime scene gloves and handed Cam another pair as she said, "Give me a hand Cam. Let's get him on his back."

As soon as he was rolled over, Mary asked, "Handsome young man. Do you recognize him, Cam?" asked Mary.

"Yeah, it's as I suspected. The victim is Joseph Cotton. He was reported missing last night after an argument with another member of the theatrical group staying at the hotel," replied Cam shaking his head.

Mary looked shocked and turned to Cam and asked, "All three victims from the same troupe? Well, that sure can't be a coincidence."

"No Mary, it sure can't be and if this keeps up they'll be no one left to suspect. Mr. Cotton was our prime suspect before today. He was in love with the first victim and had threatened the life of the second victim just a few weeks ago. I thought last night that he had perhaps committed suicide and was going to surface somewhere downstream but I'm guessing that you're going to confirm my suspicion and tell me that this was no suicide."

Bending over and examining Joseph's cold, pale face, Mary said, "Not unless he shoved himself down this well. Have a look at his mouth, Cam. Looks like the same frothing residue we found around the mouth of Mr. Burke. I will bet my reputation that there was some type of poison involved in both these cases. I'll have the lab run a full toxicology on this victim too, as soon as I finish the autopsy. Definitely not a suicide, but then you already knew that. There's no way he could throw himself down the well and then pull the cover back over."

Cam nodded his agreement and asked, "Time of death Mary?"

"Can't be 100% with this one Cam, but I would estimate the time of death to be around midnight or a little later. I'll have a better idea after I get him back to the lab and on the slab."

After getting help from Cam and Chief Bilhams' crew, the victim was placed in the black body bag and zipped up before being placed on the gurney and rolled out to the waiting van.

Saying their goodbyes, everyone left leaving Cam and Sergeant Roberts alone with the crime investigation team to wrap up their work at the castle. The team had barely finished searching the grounds and dusting for prints when Mr. Parsons walked back in his front door followed closely by Bella.

"We're just cleaning up from the dusting, sir. I don't want to leave any obvious reminders around that may upset you wife."

"You underestimate my wife, Chief Inspector. She is made of much stronger stuff. It was just the shock of it happening in our home. She was fine by the time we reached my daughter's. Matter of fact, I had a difficult time convincing her to stay."

Cam smiled widely and said, "I am certainly glad to hear that. We'll be out of your way shortly. Two officers will be posted around your house until this investigation is over. In the meantime, I have to go give Mr. Morris the bad news."

"Was it young Mr. Cotton, Chief Inspector? Kim came to the front gate yesterday evening quite upset asking if we had seen him. " asked Mr. Parsons.

"I'm afraid it is, sir. We were actually looking for him last night because he had gone missing and considering his fragile state we felt it was best not to wait the required twenty-four hours. I don't know if you realized that he was in love with Miss Martin."

"Oh yes, Chief Inspector, it was all too obvious. The young man's eyes never left her. Couldn't for the life of me understand why she would pick Burke over him. They say some young girls are attracted to bad boys and Mr. Burke was certainly a bad boy. Good actor but nasty temper. Still, I'm sorry he's dead."

"Yes sir, three young lives cut short. Now if you'll excuse me, I better get over to the hotel. Good night Mr. Parsons and thank you for your co-operation. If you need anything at all just call 999 and we'll be right over."

It was late by the time, Cam and Sergeant Roberts walked into the hotel pub. Not all the troupe was there, considering the late hour, only Kim and Anne still sitting quietly chatting in a dimly lit corner. As soon as Kim saw Cam and Sergeant Roberts enter the pub she was on her feet and hurrying across the room to Cam.

"Have you found him? Is he OK?" she half cried.

Cam took hold of Kim's arm and gently steered her back into her chair and quietly said, "I regret to inform you that Mr. Cotton's body was recovered earlier this evening. I'm very sorry, Miss Patrick."

Kim fell sobbing into Anne's arms as she exclaimed, "I knew it. It's all my fault. He's drowned himself!"

Holding Kim tightly, Anne nodded to her fellow officers and asked, "Was he in the river then, Chief Inspector?"

"No miss, he was not and we don't believe this to be a suicide. We're treating it as another murder."

Jumping to her feet, Kim demanded, "But who would hurt Joseph? Are you sure, Chief Inspector?"

"Yes, Miss Patrick. I'm afraid we are. To the best of your knowledge, do you know of anyone who might have wished him harm?"

"No, Chief Inspector, I have to be honest with you, I thought Joseph killed Alan because he blamed him for Alicia's death and then feeling overcome with remorse killed himself. He had been so down since Alicia's death. You know, he was leaving the troupe, had his bag packed and ready to go as soon as you cleared us to leave for Chepstow."

"Now Kim, please think carefully. Last night when Joseph disappeared did you notice anyone disappearing for an extended period of time or acting strangely?"

"No sir, actually Anne and I went up to my room right after you left last night. I was emotionally drained and Anne was good enough to stay up with me almost all night."

"That's right, Chief Inspector. We never left the room all night," confirmed Anne.

"Has the rest of your group retired for the night, Miss Parks?" asked Sergeant Roberts.

Looking around the room Anne replied, "I don't know if they're in their rooms but they all disappeared upstairs about an hour ago, so I assume they went off to bed."

"That being the case, we won't wake them," said Cam as he stood to leave. "Please let Mr. Morris and the rest of the group know that we'll need to speak with each of them again. We'll be back in the morning, goodnight ladies."

Chapter 10

"Hello Cam, Mary here. We have the toxicology reports back for our first two victims and you aren't going to believe this!"

Cam was still groggy when Mary rang at 6am after a late night call from PC Parks reporting on the evening events. Rolling over and sitting on the side of the bed, Cam slipped into his slippers and shuffled into the kitchen where Helen was already pouring him a cup of coffee.

Mouthing 'thank you' to Helen, Cam took a sip of the hot liquid and asked, "Is it poison as you suspected, Mary?"

"Yes Cam, but it's the type of poison that is so unbelievable. I haven't seen a case like it before. It's all very exciting."

Cam grimaced and replied, "Somehow, I don't think our young victims would find this exciting Mary. What did the report show?"

"Wolfsbane," replied a more serious Mary.

"Wolfsbane? Are you talking about the flower, Mary?" asked Cam as he struggled to remember anything he could about the plant.

"Yes Cam, the flower. It belongs to the plant genus *Aconitum*, a group of plants which are all poisonous. The native plant, sometimes called monkshood, has large leaves with rounded lobes and purple hooded flowers. Although it can be found throughout the UK, cases of accidental poisoning are very rare. Still, people plant it in their gardens, possibly unaware of the potential hazard."

"What are the symptoms of wolfsbane poisoning?"

"They vary greatly, Cam. Some symptoms of wolfsbane poisoning include vomiting, sweating, frothing at the mouth, confusion, dizziness, numbness and tingling about the face, mouth and limbs, and a burning sensation in the abdomen. Symptoms appear within an hour of exposure and death can follow within six hours. It is one of the most toxic plants that can be found in the UK, the toxins in the plant can cause a slowing of the heart rate which can be fatal," continued Mary.

Sitting down at the kitchen table, Cam held his cup out towards Helen for a refill and said, "That could explain the froth on Mr. Burke's mouth and could also hint at the cause of Mr. Cotton's death. Do you know any gardens in the area where it is being grown?"

"Many gardens in the area grow it but the borders at Wilton Castle have quite a dramatic display of them," said Mary.

"Ok, thanks for getting back to me so quickly, Mary," replied Cam.

Mary continued, "I'll have a written report on your desk later today and Cam there is something else."

"Yes, what is it Mary?"

"Whoever did this sure knows their flowers and another thing, Cam these findings would change the timeline for the alibis. The victims would have been poisoned at least six hours before they actually died and once they were dead, the killer or killers could return at any time to put Miss Martin in the Wye and Mr. Burke in the church."

"So that would make the time of poisoning of Miss Martin and Mr. Burke between 5-6pm. That would perhaps make them incapacitated or dead, depending on the dosage, sometime shortly after. So we're looking for someone who had knowledge of wolfsbane and had opportunity to poison the victims between 5-

6pm and later had time to dispose of the bodies," said Cam.

"That would seem like the likely scenario, Cam. Just keep in mind, that poison is similar to alcohol in some respects; by this I mean that a smaller person like Miss Martin would have died sooner than Mr. Burke, So it's possible that they ingested the poison at the same time.".

"Thanks again, Mary. I'll have Sergeant Roberts go over their statements again when I get into the station. In the meantime, please don't mention these findings to anyone."

"That goes without saying, Cam. Give Ilelen my love and tell her I'll stop by tomorrow with some eggs for her. I'll speak to you later and Cam, be careful, the killer's murdered three people so one more won't matter."

The best part of the morning, Sergeant Roberts went over the interviews methodically eliminating one troupe member after another. At the end of three hours of reviewing testimonies, he knocked on Cam's door and said, "Sir, I must be missing something or Mary's timeline is off because according to the interviews with the troupe and my interview with the landlord, everyone was being served dinner in the pub between 5pm and 6pm."

"OK, so the landlord says he was serving them dinner from 5-6pm but I'm sure he didn't have time to stand about just watching them for an hour. We'll need to go speak to them all again. Anne called late last night and reported that after she and Kim had gone to their room, Kim mentioned that Mr. Morris was outside talking to the couple the night they announced their engagement just before they seemed to argue then disappeared. That would make him the last person in the group to see them alive, so we'll need to ask him about their conversation. Bring the statements and let's get over there and see what we can find out," said Cam.

Entering the hotel, Cam and Sergeant Roberts headed straight to the pub hoping to find at least some of the acting troupe there. Despite the early hour, Kim sat alone, lost in her thoughts, drinking a glass of what appeared to be cider. Despite their noisy approach, Kim didn't look up until Cam's pulling out the chair across the stone floor made a loud scraping noise. As soon as he saw her eyes, Cam realized that this wasn't the first drink of the day for Kim.

"Good morning Kim," said Cam staring into her red rimmed eyes.

"Not really Chief Inspector. Would you join me in a drink? I've been toasting Joseph," slurred Kim lifting her glass in a toast.

"No thanks Kim, a bit early for me. I was wondering if you might be able to tell me about the last time that you saw Alicia and Alan again," asked Cam.

"I told you before Inspector. They announced their engagement and everyone had a toast with what we were already drinking and then they went outside. Oh yeah, did I tell you that Mr. Morris said that an engagement called for champagne and went to the bar and got a bottle and two glasses and took it out to them. He should stick to his flower-gathering; because he sure can't open a bottle of champagne, bloody fool sprayed it all over the place. He was out there talking for a while, and then the fool dropped the bottle when he opened the door to come back in, so none of us had any. It wasn't long after that when Alicia and Alan had the argument and stormed off."

144

"Flower-gathering, Kim?" asked Cam.

"Yeah, he used to be a professor of botany and was always snipping those blue flowers over at the castle. Stealing them for their seeds, I guess. He was always shoving them in his pockets."

Suddenly Cam was on his feet, "Kim, where's Anne?"

"Oh her, well old Morris thinks she should audition for the lead in Romeo and Juliet, he reckons she'd be a better draw then me, prettier you see, so they've gone over to the castle to see if her voice will carry from the tower."

Turning to Sergeant Roberts, Cam yelled as he took off running towards the castle, "My God, we've got to get to PC Parks. She's in grave danger."

"You go around by the gate and I'll go along the river in case he tries to get away," called Roberts as he took off towards the river.

Cam frantically pushed the buzzer but when there was no answer, he grabbed the top and managed to scale the gate landing roughly on the other side. Slowly getting to his feet, he limped as quickly as his injured leg would allow. As Cam rounded the corner of the first of the remaining castle ruins, Sergeant Roberts was sprinting across the garden lawns heading for the doorway of the tower. Looking up towards the tower balcony, Cam held his breath as he saw the half limp figure of PC Anne Parks being held dangerously close to the edge of the tower balcony.

Slowly positioning himself close to the foot of the balcony, Cam called out, "There is no way to escape Morris. Give yourself up! Don't make it worse by harming a police officer. Come on down and let's talk about this."

"It's too late for that. The poison is beginning to do its job and I'm not spending the rest of my life locked away, Chief Inspector," yelled Morris as he wrapped his arms around PC Parks waist.

"It's still time to save her, Morris. She hasn't done anything to you. She's just been doing her job," continued Cam trying to keep Morris talking in hopes that Sergeant Roberts could reach them in time.

"And that's what I was trying to do but those stupid kids had no respect for the theater and no respect for me. They were just going to abandon me and I just couldn't have that happen again," screamed Morris as he tightly wrapped his arms around Anne's waist.

Suddenly, Sergeant Roberts' figure appeared behind Morris on the balcony but just as he reached out to grab Morris, the cornered man threw himself off the balcony taking the young PC with him.

Moving quickly to try to save his young officer, Cam tried desperately to break her fall but Morris held onto her tight until the moment of impact.

Leaning over the balcony and watching in horror, Sergeant Roberts was already on his phone to emergency services calling for an ambulance as Cam lifted PC Parks off the inert body of Morris.

"Is she going to make it, sir?" asked Roberts.

"She's unconscious but I hope so. She was very lucky that his body broke her fall. I just hope the antidote for the poison works and it hasn't caused permanent damage. Didn't do much for him though," said Cam as he looked down at the pool of blood slowly seeping from Morris' head.

"The Parsons aren't home so run and open the gate for the ambulance. I'll stay with Anne," said Cam as he continued to cradle the young PC in his arms.

Still holding Anne in his arms, Cam reached over and felt for a vein in Morris's neck. Feeling a slight pulse, Cam silently prayed that Morris would survive so he would have to answer for his crimes in a court of law.

The ambulance arrived quickly followed immediately by Mary ready to examine what she assumed was another corpse. As Cam was assisting the ambulance crew with Anne, Mary was already examining the prone body of Morris.

"My word Cam, he's still alive."

149

"Yes, I know Mary. I've called for a helicopter to airlift him to Hereford. He wouldn't survive an ambulance ride and I think if he's to survive he'll need their specialist care," replied Cam as he scanned the sky for an incoming helicopter.

"You're right, of course. You realize that from the looks of his head injuries that there's a good chance he won't survive."

Cam just nodded as Mary continued, "Sergeant Roberts must have assumed that he was already deceased because he phoned me right after phoning for the emergency services."

"I thought so too Mary until I felt a pulse in his neck," replied Cam as he watched the ambulance crew load the still unconscious officer into the back of the ambulance.

Calling to Sergeant Roberts, Cam asked, "Can you wait here with Mary until the helicopter arrives and gets Morris? I want to ride with Anne to the hospital."

"Yes sir,'" replied Roberts as he looked at the worried face of his boss.

As Cam climbed into the back of the ambulance with Anne he could just make out the soft whop-whop-whop-whop of the approaching air ambulance. Settling himself, he watched as the paramedic ran an IV line and began calling Anne's vitals to the hospital staff awaiting her arrival at A&E. There was little left for Cam to do but hold the young PC's hand and pray for her recovery. He knew that she was just doing the job she was trained to do and had volunteered for, but Cam still couldn't shake the feeling of guilt for not suspecting Morris earlier. During the fifteen-minute drive to the hospital, Cam went over every detail of the case in his head and admonished himself for missed clues to the murderer.

It was a full day and night before PC Anne Parks finally opened her eyes to find a dozing, unshaven and disheveled Chief Inspector Fergus sitting beside her bed with his head in his hands.

"How long have I been unconscious, Chief Inspector?" asked Anne in a soft voice.

Jerking awake, Cam replied as he pressed the buzzer to call the nurse, "Thank God. We've been so worried. You've been out for nearly 48 hours, Anne."

"Am I going to be alright?" asked Anne has her hands began to run down her body checking for injuries.

Smiling Cam replied, "The doctors say you'll make a full recovery."

"He must have put something in my coffee, sir. All I remember is him talking about Romeo and Juliet and then I got agitated and we went outside. The next thing I remember is feeling a bit faint and then nothing until I just woke up here," continued Anne.

Cam reached over and patted her hand and said, "Yes, Morris had concocted a poison that he could slip into drinks from wolfsbane and that's what he had given you and our three victims. Depending on the dosage it causes confusion, irritation and slowly lowers the heart rate until death occurs. You were very lucky that the doctors knew what he had given you."

"How did the doctors know? Did he confess?" asked Anne.

"No, he didn't tell us what he had used. You were lucky that Mary Hamilton got the toxicology results back on the first two victims

153

before Morris decided to get rid of you too," replied Cam.

"I really didn't suspect him Chief Inspector. To be honest, I didn't think he had murder in him. He seemed so docile and almost child-like at times. I hope he's in custody now and is made to pay for his crimes."

Cam didn't reply. He saw no reason to bring up Anne's narrow escape from being plunged off the tower until she was feeling better. Pressing the bedside call button, Cam informed the nurses' station that their patient was awake and talking.

Within minutes a young doctor entered the room and began checking Anne's vitals and smiling at her confirming what Cam had just said, "You're going to be quite stiff and sore for a few weeks and I would suggest that you stay off work for at least two weeks. No operating machinery or driving please until you are back for your follow-up in a fortnight, understand?"

Giving him a mock salute, Anne replied, "Yes sir! Now when can I get out of here?"

"Is tomorrow soon enough for you, Miss Parks?" asked the doctor as he started for the door.

"Today would be better," called Anne at the retreating back of the doctor.

Cam's smiling face suddenly turned serious as he stared at the bruised and swollen face of his young constable and said, "The doctor said at least two weeks recovery but I am thinking you should be out the entire month and go home to your family to recover. Before you object, you've done an excellent job PC Parks and you deserve to have a chance to recover surrounded by loved ones. So no arguments, understand?"

155

"If you're sure that it won't leave you under-staffed. The doctor did say I'd be alright in two weeks and he does want to see me back then."

Turning his back and walking to the door to finally end his vigil at Anne's bedside, Cam replied, "I said no arguments. The department has done without both of us for two days so I'm sure it will survive. It's an order and I'll have the doctor reschedule your appointment, besides if you have any medical issues there's no shortage of doctors in York. Now, you get some rest. I'll be back in the morning before you're discharged and arrange for your transport back home to York and your parents but right now I want to get home and shower and shave before checking in at the station."

When there was no reply from Anne, Cam turned back around to find that the young PC had already fallen back asleep and softly closing the door behind him headed for home.

156

Chapter 11

Heading down the hospital corridor, Cam pulled out his mobile and phoned home to let Helen know he would be stopping by long enough to shower, shave and change clothes before going into the station. As usual, when he arrived home fifteen minutes later he found Helen bustling about in the kitchen. Placing a quick kiss on her cheek, he headed into the bedroom where he found a fresh set of clothes laid out on the bed and his shaving kit set out in the bathroom. Smiling to himself, he thought, 'There's none like her.' His belief was confirmed when fifteen minutes later he walked back into the kitchen to see the table set with a fry-up and steaming coffee waiting for him.

Pulling out the chair and sitting down opposite her husband, Helen asked, "So, no permanent adverse effects of the poisoning?"

"The doctors' confirm that all tests show there is no damage to any organs from the poison but she'll need to have a minimum of a fortnight of rest. I'm having her driven back to York for a month so she can be with her parents during her recovery," said Cam between bites of his toast.

"I am so glad, Cam. I knew when you stayed at the hospital that it was very bad and when Mary came by with the eggs yesterday she told me about the poison and what had happened over at the Castle. I imagine the Parsons are absolutely mortified that such nasty crimes have been committed in their home and on their property. Lucky Mrs. Parsons used to be with MI5 or it might have greatly affected her."

Raising an eyebrow Cam said, "I didn't know that, but her husband did tell me that she was made of stronger stuff when I expressed my concern for her being upset."

"Oh yes, from what Mary told me, she had quite an illustrious career, only retiring when she and her husband began the restoration. Mr. Parsons' business requires him to travel a lot and apparently despite her age, she's a crack shot and more than capable of taking care of herself. Helen reckoned had she been home that morning that she would have taken Morris out before he had a chance to leap from the tower with poor PC Parks," remarked Helen.

Finishing his coffee, Cam shook his head and said, "My detective skills must be getting dulled. I would never have suspected. Now I look even more forward to visiting the Parsons again as soon as this investigation is wrapped-up. Now, I'm off to the station. Mary phoned while I was in the bedroom changing and she's probably already there waiting for me. Apparently, she has some information that she thinks may be helpful."

159

Opening the door to leave, Cam turned and smiled at his wife as he said, "Thanks for a wonderful breakfast. Don't prepare anything for dinner tonight. I want to take the best wife a man could have out to dinner."

A quick walk to the station got Cam to the parking lot just as Mary was climbing down from her ancient Land Rover.

"Morning Cam," shouted Mary. "I hear PC Parks is being released tomorrow. Great news!"

Smiling brightly, Cam replied, "Yes, it is. I've got to arrange for her transport back to her parents in York tomorrow after she is released. The doctors understandably don't want her driving."

As they walked across the drive and up the steps together, Mary asked, "Any updates on Morris from Hereford Hospital yet?"

Opening the door for Mary, Cam shook his head, "Nothing as of this morning so far. Last night he was still unconscious and they weren't hopeful that he would ever regain consciousness. So, we may never understand what drove him to commit the murders, other than what he said at the tower about being angry about them leaving the theatrical company. Surely, there has to be more to it."

"People have murdered for less, Cam," was Mary's only response as she shook her head in disbelief and walked down the hall to file her final report.

"I still can't believe that just losing some of his troupe would be enough for him to murder three people and jump from that tower taking Anne with him," called Cam after her as he walked into the incident room.

Before he could even get settled at his desk, Sergeant Roberts appeared at the door waving a stack of what appeared to be faxes.

"Sir, I've spent all morning checking into Mr. Morris' background and I think you'll find these reports very interesting."

Reaching out his hand for the thick stack of faxed reports, Cam asked, "Thanks, can you give me the gist of what they say?"

Pulling up a chair and facing his boss, the young sergeant eagerly began, "It seems that Mr. Morris was previously a married man and has two adult children. According to their neighbors and staff at the university where he taught it was not a happy marriage. Mrs. Morris was the one unhappy in the marriage and made no secret of it."

Growing impatient Cam asked, "Having an unhappy wife doesn't explain his behavior Sergeant. I'm sure that she was well-pleased

162

that he was traveling and away from home most of the summer."

"Well sir, I'm sure she would have been, if she was still alive. Seems she died very suddenly, apparent heart failure after a bout with the flu. I've managed to contact a neighbor of theirs trying to get the next of kin and was told that neither children would have anything to do with their father after the mother's death. I did manage to get some addresses for them and was planning on contacting them after we spoke."

"Sergeant, go see if Mary is still down the hall filing her report and tell her I need to speak to her urgently."

"Yes sir."

As soon as Mary and Sergeant Roberts were back in the incident room, Cam said, "Mary, can you explain to us one more time how wolfsbane poisoning affects someone?"

"Sure Cam, some symptoms of wolfsbane poisoning include vomiting, sweating, frothing at the mouth, confusion, dizziness, numbness and tingling about the face, mouth and limbs, and a burning sensation in the abdomen. The toxins in the plant can cause a slowing of the heart rate which can be fatal."

"So, if a woman was being treated for the flu and died of a heart attack and no one suspected poison, could a poisoner get away with it?"

Mary shrugged and said, "Quite possibly Cam. If there was no apparent reason to suspect poisoning and the victim had a history of heart problems then no one might question the death."

Looking over at Roberts, Cam asked, "Does the report indicate anything else?"

"Yes sir, it notes that the deceased was under a doctor's care for Angina."

Looking confused, Mary asked, "Are you trying to suggest that Morris has done this before?"

Nodding, Cam replied, "Quite possibly Mary. It would seem that after his wife died, his adult children refused to have anything to do with him. We'll need to speak with them to see if the reason for this abandonment of their father is that they suspected him of causing their mother's death."

Mary sat quietly for a moment seemingly lost in her own thoughts then solemnly replied, "If this is true, it might explain why Morris acted so irrationally when his actors told him what they were leaving the production. The idea that his own children would have nothing to do with him after his wife's death must have affected him greatly. If he was, in fact, innocent of any wrong doing in her death, I can't imagine the damage it would have done to him psychologically to have his own children believe he murdered their mother."

"You almost sound like you feel sorry for him, Mary," replied Cam.

"No Cam, I don't feel sorry for him. He's taken three innocent lives and tried to kill PC Parks but I would hate for him to die before we can determine if he did murder his wife. If he's innocent of at least that, then I think his children need to know. I think we need to get an order to exhume Mrs. Morris' remains so it can be tested as quickly as possible."

"I agree Mary. I'll petition the court immediately and tell them it's urgent," said Cam as he reached for the phone.

Chapter 12

Morris remained in a medically induced coma for four days giving Cam time to convince the man's son and daughter to come to Hereford. It had taken quite some persuading for them to even consider coming to the bedside of the man they felt was responsible for their mother's death.

On the morning of the fifth day while Cam was at home finishing breakfast, an urgent call came from the hospital informing him that Morris was awake. Leaving his half-eaten breakfast on the table, Cam was out the door and racing the sixteen miles to Hereford.

Calling his sergeant to meet him at the hospital as he raced through the corridors to Morris' room, he was informed that the reports of Mrs. Morris' wife had just been received. Telling him to bring them to the hospital immediately, Cam hurried to Morris' room in the Critical Care Unit and was met by a group of doctors just exiting.

Before Cam could utter a word, the doctor-in-charge grimly said, "I've just informed Mr. Morris that there is no hope for recovery. We have brought him out of a medically induced coma at the request of his children. I am just going to inform them that their father is awake and has agreed to see them. He has requested to speak with you first, but I must inform you that a nurse will be present at all times and under no circumstances will we allow a dying man to be distressed any more than necessary, understood Chief Inspector?"

"Of course doctor, I understand completely," replied Cam as he pushed the door open and entered the room nodding at the nurse who stood poised at the side of the bed watching the monitors recording Morris' vitals.

Sitting down in the chair beside Morris' bed, Cam asked, "How are you Mr. Morris?"

Turning his still swollen face to look at Cam, Morris slurred, "I've just been told by the good doctors that I'm going to die Chief Inspector but at least I won't end my remaining days in prison. I couldn't survive in there, you understand. I suppose you are here to get what they call a "death-bed confession.""

"Actually no, Mr. Morris what you admitted at the tower was confession enough and besides if what the doctor's say is true it is all irrelevant now isn't it? I would like to know why, though."

Growing very quiet for a moment, Mr. Morris replied, "Did you know that when a person is in a coma that their brain is still active Chief Inspector? I could hear everything going on around me and I was able to think clearly for the first time in a very long time. You see when my wife died, my son and daughter felt I had done something to hasten her death and they refused to speak to me again. I admit that my wife and I argued a lot and she threatened

169

to leave me over the years but I did love her. I swear to you now that I didn't harm her. I heard from neighbors that I am a grandfather. Do you know how hurtful that can be, knowing that you'll never see your children again or meet your grandchildren? Well, I know now that's no excuse for the horrible things that I have done."

Thinking of his son in New Zealand and his daughter, Cam couldn't begin to imagine the pain and anxiety he would feel if they just cut him out of their lives completely. .

A soft knock on the door, announced the arrival of Sergeant Roberts. Peeping his head in the door, he asked, "Sir, can I see you a minute?"

"I'll be right back, Mr. Morris. Try to rest."

Nodding again to the nurse, Cam walked out into the hall where Roberts stood waiting, envelope in hand, with the head doctor and Morris' son and daughter.

Clearing this throat, Cam reached his hand out for the envelope holding the report of their mother's post mortem results and addressing Morris' children said, "As you know, we had your mother's body exhumed for examination into the cause of her death. It is my understanding that you have been estranged from your father because you believed he had poisoned her. I have just taken a death bed statement from your father stating he loved your mother and had no hand in her death and I believe these results will confirm that he is telling the truth. He has no reason to lie now."

Handing the envelope to Morris' son, Cam signaled Sergeant Roberts to follow him to the waiting area outside the unit and watched as the son read the report and passed it to his sister.

Wiping the tears streaming down her cheek with the back of her hand, Morris' daughter turned and looked back to Cam and mouthed

171

"thank you" before taking her brother's arm and following the doctor into their father's room to say their final goodbyes.

An exhausted Sergeant Roberts sat very quietly with his head in his hands for a while before saying, "Do you really think that the events in a person's past life can warp them so much that they would turn him into a cold-blooded murderer?"

"I'm afraid so, events in our past definitely determine how we will turn out in the future. Drug addicts don't start out saying, 'I'm going to become addicted to drugs when I grow up.' Events and circumstances can so terribly affect an individual that they will commit heinous crimes that they could never have conceived themselves possible of just years before."

Cam's conversation with his Sergeant was soon interrupted by the doctor exiting Morris' room and making his way to where they sat waiting.

"Chief Inspector, Mr. Morris passed away a few minutes ago. His children are still in there composing themselves. I'm afraid it was a very traumatic farewell for them based on their behavior since their mother's death."

Nodding his understanding, Cam replied, "I can only imagine."

Continuing, the doctor said, "Mr. Morris' last words were for you, Chief Inspector. He asked me to thank you for what you have done for him today and tell you that he is filled with remorse for his actions and prays your officer will make a full recovery."

Chapter 13

Two weeks passed and Cam and Helen once again found themselves sitting on the banks of the Wye enjoying a picnic. This time they sat in the shadow of the ruins of Wilton Castle as guests of the Parson's. The weather was refreshing after three days of uncommonly hot and humid weather and the breeze off the river reminded Cam of the much cooler weather of his Scottish home. Cam sat quietly stroking the ever-present Bella, lost in his own private world, still full of guilt for not suspecting Morris before more lives were lost.

While Helen was taken on a tour of the gardens by Mr. Parsons, Mrs. Parsons sat quietly observing her guest before saying in a soft voice, "I can tell that you are still thinking about the deaths of those young people. You know you can speak to me about your case if you'd like. After all, I did sign the Official Secrets Act and I worked as a profiler for many years. Perhaps, I could help you understand that none of this was your fault."

Before Cam could respond, the kindly woman said, "I had a case, similar to yours many years ago and despite working nonstop for thirty-six hours, I wasn't able to target the perpetrator before he managed to kill four innocent children. For months I had nightmares about those children and I spent my off hours going over all the available clues to see what I had missed. In the end, there was nothing. He had no previous record. There was no reason to suspect him and to make matters worse there were three other suspects that had opportunity, motive and no alibi. Once I came to realize that I had done the best I could with what facts that I had, the nightmares stopped."

Gazing up into the kind eyes of this wise woman, Cam replied, "You're right of course. I have been going over and over every detail in my mind. And you're correct. There was absolutely no reason to suspect Morris until just moments before he jumped from your tower. The nightmares have stopped now, but I wonder if I will ever be able to look at this river the same way again."

Reaching over and placing a hand on Cam's arm, she replied, "The Wye didn't take that poor girl's life, any more than my beautiful flowers are at fault for those young people's deaths. Nature cannot be blamed for the actions of an unbalanced mind."

Cam nodded at the wisdom of this woman as the two rose and walked across the gardens arm-in-arm to join her husband and Helen on the patio.

Over the days that followed, the memory of the Lady of the Wye began to slowly fade and the sleepy market town that had grown up on the banks of the mighty River Wye returned to normal. It was idyllic....